Milinda
DiFranzo

Long Way From Home

By Melinda Di Lorenzo

Copyright 2015, Melinda Di Lorenzo

Cover art courtesy of © Konradbak | Dreamstime.com

Dedication

To Shelley D.
Big love to you for your invaluable help and general awesomeness!

Prologue

At first when I opened my eyes, I thought I'd gone blind.

Terror coursed through me in that unremembered nightmare kind of way – when the dream hangs on, still real enough to be scary, but not so clear that you can say what it was that frightened you about it.

Breathe, I told myself. *In. Out.*

Slowly, I lifted my hand. But it was so dark that I couldn't even see the outline of it. Fear hit me again, and before I could remind myself to stay calm, I waved my fingers frantically in front of my face, desperate to see them. I couldn't.

My gaze flicked to one side, then the other. Nothing but blackness.

Oh, God.

This was no dream.

A scream built in the back of my throat, and I let it out because I had to. And it provided a momentary distraction. Because while I could feel the burn of my voice against my vocal cords, I couldn't hear the sound of it.

What the hell? I thought, suddenly more irritated than afraid.

Even though I couldn't see, I closed my eyes, sighing heavily in frustration. I made myself ignore the fact that although I could feel the air leaving my body, I couldn't hear that either.

The blackness extended to my hearing as well as my sight.

I tried to remember what the last thing I'd been doing was, but my brain felt fuzzy.

Think, Lindsay.

Had I been drinking something, maybe, that made me so forgetful?

Yes.

Vodka and orange juice to calm my nerves. I'd taken a big sip, then put my head down awkwardly on a lumpy pillow.

I frowned at the recollection. It didn't make any sense. My pillows at home were most definitely not lumpy.

I suddenly became aware that I *could* actually hear... something. A high-pitched whine that sounded like it was coming from all around me. I lifted my hand and placed it on my forehead. The pitch of the ringing was becoming unbearable very quickly. I covered my ears, and the noise became even worse.

"Dear God," I muttered.

The sound was coming from *inside* rather than from outside.

I shook my head, and the shrillness reverberated back and forth with the movement.

Should I stand up? I thought, and then added wryly, *Even though I just realized that I'm sitting down.*

I opened my eyes again and strained against the darkness, willing myself to see. I tipped my head back and found that it was resting against a soft-backed chair. I looked up, and relief overwhelmed me. I could see something at last. Pinpricks of light – stars –spread out above me.

It's nighttime, I realized. *And I'm outside.*

The knowledge was soothing, even as it was disturbing.

I tried to stand up but couldn't. Something was pushing against my hips, fixing me to the spot. I glanced down automatically, but of course still couldn't really see a damned thing in the darkness. Sighing, I used my hands in place of my eyes. I felt around my waist and found that I was wearing a nylon lap belt. I ran my fingers along the cinched strap until they met with a cold, metal clasp. I tried to grasp it to pull it apart, but I had trouble getting a grip, and when I finally managed to get a satisfactory hold, the clasp jammed.

"Dammit!" I shouted, and was rewarded by the sound of my own voice.

It sounded underwater and very far away at the same time, but it was still my voice. It reassured me, and I tried with renewed vigour to make my hands cooperate, but they really didn't want to do it.

I felt something warm and wet hit my wrist. I held my arm up and inhaled sharply. My eyes were finally adjusting to the dark and I could see, just a little. But it wasn't good. My hand looked like a whitish blob, and while I was momentarily thrilled to have some restored vision, I concluded immediately that the dark blotch marring the whitish blob was the source of the warm wetness.

Blood, I thought, disappointed and concerned that I hadn't felt any pain.

A rusty smell assaulted my nose, and I knew it had to be coming from the fresh slice on my hand. I breathed in the scent, glad that at least one of my senses was working at full capacity. My deep inhale brought awareness of another odor – one that reminded me of burning hair.

Panic finally set in.

Outside.

At night.

Sliced hand.

Something hair-like on fire.

My brain made the list against my will.

I grabbed the seat belt, willing it to loosen. The blood on my wrist slid down my sleeve, and I could feel it sticking to my sweater.

"Ohgodohgodohgod," I panted helplessly, over and over again.

Finally, I heard a snap and a click.

Victory.

I flung my body forward and landed on something cold and soft.

Snow. This just gets better and better.

I forced myself up onto my knees. My body ached with the effort, and I realized that I hurt all over. I closed my eyes briefly, trying to block out the pain. When I opened them again, the sky seemed marginally brighter. I frowned, wondering if my vision was getting better, or if the sun was starting to come out already.

A noise came from somewhere around me, too. I knew it was loud because it was nearly drowning out the ringing in my ears.

The sky got even lighter, and my eyes widened as I took in the bleak landscape before me.

It was snowy. Very snowy. In fact, now that I could see, I realized that I was completely surrounded by white. I glanced around frantically. Fresh fallen snow on the ground under me. Snow-covered mountains in the distance. White as far as my vision could reach.

I started to shiver, as if the realization of my surroundings directly affected my physical reaction. My teeth started to chatter, and I worked to stop them. I looked up at the sky again. I could still see the stars pinpricking through the darkness, even though there seemed to be light all around me.

I only had time to be puzzled for a second or two before a hissing pop turned my attention to the chair where I'd been stuck just minutes earlier.

It was on fire. Really on fire. The seat back was engulfed in flames already, and the cushion was smoldering. My mouth dropped open, and I scurried backwards on my hands and knees.

The other noise – the one that wasn't coming from inside my head – emanated from the burning chair, building to an intensity that made me cringe.

And then it erupted.

I gasped and threw my arms up to shield my body from the assault.

A hundred pieces of foam, fabric, and plastic exploded all around me. Bits of burning seat landed on my sweater, putting a hole right through the sleeve and scorching my arm.

There was a final, momentarily deafening pop, and the ringing in my ears subsided completely. The only sound left was the cheery crackle of an airplane seat burning to a crisp.

I stared at it forlornly, watching as bits of the seat floated down to the ground. And then the clasp of the seat belt that had given me so much trouble a few minutes earlier came flying through the air, cracked me solidly in the side of the head, making my vision swim, and the world faded away.

Six Hours Earlier…

Chapter 1

I've heard people say – on more than one occasion – that things can change in an instant. And I guess sometimes that's true. Life can blindside you. Knock you on your ass. Or make you sit up and want to live it better.

I stared out the window of the small, commercial airplane, trying to decide if it was true. I took a big sip of my vodka and orange juice, then opened and closed my free hand on the arm of my airplane seat, and reminded myself that I *knew* it was true. After all, I'd had one of those life changing moments just this past week.

Hadn't I?

For the hundredth time, I questioned whether or not it *was* a life changing moment, or if it was just a change I'd made to my life. A voluntary thing.

No. It had to be the former.

I'd made the right choice in leaving everything I knew behind. I'd made the right choice leaving *him* behind.

But doubts ran rampant through my brain, fuelled by the quiet of the overtired, red-eye crowd on the little plane. We'd been sitting on the tarmac for too long, and the free drinks offered in compensation were starting to get to me.

Was life in my urban Canadian town going to go on like I'd never been there at all? Was Ben going to keep seeing that girl, even though he said he'd stopped? Was my boss, Sadie – who also happened to be my closest friend – going to replace me inside of another week? Should I call her again, just to make sure she understood that I'd only be gone for six months?

I stifled a sigh, and forced my hands to stay away from my purse and my phone.

I'd spoken with Sadie a hundred times over the last seven days. Defending the job I'd taken. Defending my sanity.

You didn't take this contract, take this flight, and *take this leap of faith just so you could go crying to Sadie the second you had doubts,* I reminded myself.

And the last conversation had ended in me telling her that I would most definitely *not* be calling her from each airport, asking her if I should come home. In fact, I'd sworn rather adamantly that I wouldn't do more than send a postcard for the whole six months I was away. Unless I met a handsome Russian man. In which case, I'd gladly fly her out to be my maid of honor.

I smiled to myself and took another sip of my drink.

That particular claim had earned me a snorting laugh from Sadie. She'd said it would be just like me to run away from one wedding only to jump straight into another.

Choosing a path and committing to it is something I've always been terrible at.

Flat or heels? Crisis.

Salad or fries? It'll eat me up for a week.

Get married? Or run away screaming? Let a flight across the world help that one along.

But second guessing…that, I have down to an art. It's one of two talents I possess. Fine-tuned. And as equally useless in most situations as the first.

Lindsay Stott, language savant, bad decision maker.

Try putting *that* on your resume. Or better yet, try having it engraved on a door hanger for your office.

I smiled a little to myself. *Well. At least I can piggyback the second onto the first, and question every decision I make in four languages instead of one.*

And soon it would be five languages. Which excited me in spite of my trepidation about every other little thing.

Put me in a room full of people who spoke perfect English, and I would become a stuttering fool. But send me into a crowd of non-English speakers, and I was completely at ease. Give me an hour with those people, and I'd have picked up a dozen or more words and phrases. A week of contact, and I'd be able to carry on a conversation.

Once, Ben had asked me if I had an eidetic memory, and I'd laughed and accused him of scouring the Internet for an explanation he would never find.

"It's not something I *do*," I'd told him. "It's something I *am*."

I was looking forward to *being* that part of myself again. To becoming an anonymous face in a new town and immersing myself in a language and culture I'd never experienced. To adding Russian to my repertoire, which already included fluent French, Punjabi, and Italian, along with a smattering of Hungarian, Tagalog, and Mandarin.

And on top of that, there was the bed and breakfast I'd reserved to look forward to. The VRBO photo had shown it in the wintertime. It was a gingerbread-esque house with a toasty-looking wood fireplace and a handmade quilt on the queen-sized bed. I could almost smell the homemade buns cooking in the frosty morning.

I hadn't second guessed that part of my decision. Not one bit.

My eyes found the frosted window again, and I willed time to speed up, just a little.

This little blip was the last major stop on my twenty-nine hour journey. Toronto to London. London to here. Then Frankfurt to Moscow. Now I sat inside the smaller plane that would take me to the more remote area of the Kola Peninsula. From there, a charter flight would carry me from Murmansk to Krasnoshchelye.

I'd spend the next half a year there, first learning the language, then helping a university professor with some translations. Where I could stop thinking about Ben, and the choice I'd made to leave him.

Except it wasn't really a choice, was it?

He hadn't been the man of my dreams. Not at all. What he was, was *every* woman's dream. Smart and handsome. A little bit wild. But tempered by an overbearing mother to whom he was sweetly devoted. And it begged to be tamed completely. By the *right* woman.

He had all that going for him, plus a good job, a sense of humor, and a complete inability to find negativity in life.

So what's not to love about that?

The answer is easy. Nothing.

So I did it. I loved him. Enough that I made the choice. I agreed to marry him.

But my talent kicked in, and I second guessed it all.

I sent him packing.

I could lie and say it was because of his affair. It would be easy to believe. It was probably what nearly every person who heard the story assumed.

Scorned woman kicks womanizing man to the curb.

But the truth is, that's not the order in which things happened. Just the opposite, in fact.

If I had to sum up the conversation, it would look a little like this:

Me: I can't marry you, Ben.

Him: I slept with Amber from work.

Me: Okay. Here's your collection of DVDs.

There was some more stuff in there. Some questions from Ben about why I'd waited until we already signed the lease agreement for our apartment and paid for my dress. (I didn't have a good answer.) And queries from me about whether or not Amber was a regular thing or a one-time thing. (His reply was the one that would make people assume that his cheating *was* the motivating factor for ending our relationship.)

But weirdly, none of that made me mad, or sad. A bit guilty, maybe. But mostly, the cold-feet cliché clicked just right for me. Like a key in lock.

And it opened the door for me. The door that led to the kick-in-the-pants, life changing moment. With no more time for second guessing.

As if sensing the finality of my thoughts, the captain made a muffled announcement in Russian, and the plane started rolling.

I buckled my seat belt carefully and gripped the armrests as we took off. A smiling flight attendant handed me a package of crackers and a bottle of water, and I took both gratefully.

After sixteen hours of off-and-on, alcohol-induced sleep, the two-hour trip from Moscow to Murmansk made me feel tense. I tapped my foot anxiously until the passenger in front of me turned around and gave me a dirty look. I tried to focus instead on my book of common Russian phrases. It was written both phonetically and in the Russian alphabet, but it still wasn't much help. Even though I'd briefly studied the Russian alphabet in university, and had memorized a lot of it, I hated trying to learn a language from a book.

"Spasibo," I muttered out loud. "Kak u vas dela?"

I closed the book. I had no idea if I was saying the words correctly. I needed to hear them. I reminded myself that I only had one more flight to go before I got to the cozy bed and breakfast. And then I would have all the Russian I could handle.

Someone tapped me on the shoulder.

"Business or pleasure?" asked a friendly, female voice with a British accent.

"Business," I replied without turning around.

I heard the unbuckling of a seat belt, and in a moment, a pretty blonde woman plopped herself down in the seat beside me.

"I'm Anna," she said.

"Lindsay," I greeted.

"You staying in Murmansk?" she asked.

"No," I told her. "I'm taking a charter plane to some place called..."

I paused, trying to remember the name of the town. My mind had gone temporarily blank.

"Krasnoshchelye?" Anna filled in.

"That's the one."

"You've been before?"

"Nope. First time in Russia."

"And you chose the Kola Peninsula?" she laughed. "Are you running *from* a man? Or *to* a man?"

"Both," I told her.

I explained about the man named Dr. Adam Demidov and his translation project. I told her about my talent for languages. But I was careful to leave out the details about Ben. Being a runaway tends to put a damper on new friendships. And God knew I was going to need new friends.

"So you picked the professor?" she asked. "You are one brave woman."

"You've met him, then?"

"No. I learned my own Russian at school. I teach English to seventh and eighth graders in Krasnoshchelye," she replied. "But Professor Demidov has a reputation amongst my students."

"Should I be scared?" I asked.

"Maybe," she admitted with a smile.

I liked her already.

"Are you going to be on my charter?" I wondered hopefully.

"Yes," she told me. "And I'll give you my number before we land. Then you can call me when you get sick of the professor. We can grab a drink. And you can tell me, also, about the man you're running from."

I winced a little at the thought of talking about Ben.

"That would take a lot more than one drink," I told her.

Anna grinned and pulled a bottle of clear liquid out of her purse.

"Interested?"

"Russian vodka?"

"None other. And they'll let us open it on the charter," she said.

"Hmm. Do you have any orange juice in that purse?" I asked, and Anna laughed.

"This flight will be short. Then I'll see what I can dig up."

***

She was right. Just a few hours later we were already dragging our suitcases across the tarmac in the dark, me struggling to keep up with a very sure-footed Anna. I held my sweater as tightly as I could against my body, and wished that I thought to grab my parka from my bag. It was windy, freezing, and very hard to see. My miniscule bit of research had warned me about the cold, but it couldn't have prepared me for this.

"I thought that Murmansk was supposed to be ice free," I said through chattering teeth.

"Ice free isn't storm free. And wait until we get to Krasnoshchelye. Some days it's so cold you can barely leave the house," Anna replied cheerfully.

"That's what I hear."

We handed our bags to a man standing at the bottom of the short wheeled staircase that led up to the charter plane.

Anna shot me a smile as we climbed up. "Let me ask you something…What time do you think it is?"

I squinted against the pitch black.

"Midnight?" I guessed, trying unsuccessfully to calculate how long I'd been travelling and what the time difference was between here and home.

My new friend grinned. "It's two in the afternoon. You'll never get used to the dark, so don't bother asking how we do it."

"All right," I agreed.

I knew about the polar nights, of course, but that didn't make it any less disconcerting.

Two in the afternoon, and pitch black.

I followed Anna into the plane, where the Britishwoman took off her coat, and motioned for me to sit with her. I obliged, and decided immediately that I liked the little plane. Mostly because it didn't look much like a plane at all. Instead of rows, it had four wide seats that swivelled to face each other, and there was a small table between them.

After a moment, two more women entered the plane and greeted Anna excitedly in Russian. They stashed their bags and joined us.

"Vera and Anfisa are the wives of some local importers," Anna told me.

"Shopping trip," one of the women said, shaking her bags for emphasis.

"A successful shopping trip," the other woman added.

"Excellent English," Anna said.

"You teach us well," the first woman stated as they settled themselves.

"You taught them? Maybe I should've hired you instead of Adam Demidov," I suggested.

"I'd rather be your friend than be correcting your grammar," Anna replied.

The plane jerked to a start without warning, and I buckled my seat belt quickly in response. Anna grinned at me as we bumped along and began a rapid and excessively uneven ascent.

"These rides can be rough," she warned. "But at least we're going up in style."

The wind smacked against the sides of the plane, making the windows shake. We climbed higher and higher, and I gritted my teeth because the ride wasn't getting any smoother.

The captain's voice – guttural and in Russian to boot – cut in over the roar of the engine.

"What did he say?" I asked anxiously.

Anna shrugged. "There's a storm with heavy winds so he's going to alter our course a bit to compensate. Takes longer, but it will be less bumpy."

The plane vibrated against the turbulence, and I swallowed nervously. It worried me that *this* was the less bumpy option.

Anna patted my hand. "Vodka now?"

"God, yes."

Anna reached under the table and helped herself to some glasses. Then she turned to the Russian women and asked them a question. One of them nodded, and to my delight, she dug out a carton of orange juice from one of her bags.

I downed the first screwdriver in one gulp and held out my glass for another.

"Budem zdorovi!" said one of the Russian woman in an approving voice.

"What does that mean?" I asked.

"It best translates as, *cheers*!" said Anna and poured us a second round.

I tried out the phrase. "Budem zdorovi!"

"Good," said the Russian woman.

"Very good," Anna agreed.

"Budem zdorovi," I repeated, raising my glass.

It was the perfect phrase to symbolize my new beginning.

But the plane dipped suddenly, and thoughts of celebrating the successful break from my old life went out of my head as I almost lost my drink. One of the Russian women did spill hers, and unbuckled to clean up the mess. She excused herself to use the restroom and my stomach flipped uncomfortably I watched her make her way to the rear of the plane.

I looked away, swallowed the rest of my vodka and orange juice, and pressed my head against the window. The glass felt icy and way too brittle to feel safe.

"Do you want a pillow?" Anna asked.

"That probably wouldn't be a bad idea," I admitted.

"You get used to the ride after taking it a few times," she told me sympathetically. "My first time I actually threw up."

She stood up and grabbed a lumpy pillow from the tiny compartment above our heads. When she handed it to me, I put it between the chilly window and my face. I felt the glass shudder anyway, and I shifted so that I'd be resting against something more stable. But the side of the plane was shuddering, too. Anna was just retaking her seat when the whole thing lurched sideways suddenly.

My torso bent away from the window, but my lower body was held in place by the seat belt. From the corner of my eye, I saw Anna stumble in the aisle. A frightened scream came from the back of the plane, and I cringed, thinking of the Russian woman stuck inside the tiny restroom.

The plane tipped the other way then, and suddenly, shockingly, we were upside down. Anna landed on the roof with a sickening crack. The screaming from the rear of the plane stopped abruptly, and we righted again almost immediately. Anna flew back down, hitting a seat in the row directly beside me. Her eyes were rolled back in her head, and a gash the width of my thumb cut across her cheek.

Oh God!

My heart beat frantically in my chest, and I couldn't make my mouth form any words. The scene unfolding around me didn't seem real.

The plane tossed back and forth relentlessly. And then a pop resounded through the cabin. A trickle of freezing cold air tickled my neck, and the cabin shuddered.

I tried to force my head to swivel toward the source of the cold air, but dizziness assaulted me, and I couldn't move.

The world seemed to buck, and with a thump, I cracked my head against the window. Everything disappeared in a howling storm, and I plunged into a nightmare of ice and cold and white as far as the eye could see.

Chapter Two

Fight!
The command came from in my head.
Okay.
The response was quieter, but internal, too.
Inventory.
Two legs. *Yes.*
Two arms. *Yes.*
If you can feel them, you can move them.
I wanted to wake up, and I couldn't do it.
Awareness was a stuttering thing.
I was finally warm.
That helped.
But I shouldn't be warm.
That was a bad thing.
Fight!
Except I couldn't remember why I was fighting.
And that wasn't just bad. It was life threatening. I knew it.
God help me.
It was a prayer, not a curse.
I felt the struggle, inside and out, but couldn't make real sense of it.
My mind refused to focus.
I'm not asleep, I thought. *So why won't my eyes open?*
I could almost see something against my still lids.
Lightness against the darkness.
I willed my eyes to open, and they wouldn't.
I wasn't supposed to be lying there. I knew that. And not much else.

***

I'd been dreaming the most pleasant dream.
My mother.

Ben.
Sadie.
I frowned.

Something wasn't quite right. It wasn't a dream. It was a not-too-distant memory, and I didn't think that it had ended pleasantly.

Russia.
The plane crash.

Ah, I thought, finally figuring it out. *That was my life, flashing before my eyes.*

I slipped out of consciousness again, and I welcomed the retreat.

***

Fight!

The insistent voice shouted again, and at last I obeyed. I dragged myself out of the hazy darkness and forced my eyes open.

I'm cold, I thought, and shivered involuntarily. *Really cold.*

I groaned. Something airy and wet was hitting my face.

Snow.

And then I remembered where I was. Or I remembered that I didn't know where I was, depending how I chose to look at the situation.

I spat out a mouthful of melting snow, then rolled onto my back.

I stared up at the sky.

It was starting to come down hard, and in seconds, the stars were blotted out by the clouds.

I glanced to the side and spotted the offending seat belt that had cracked me on the temple. I also saw that what was left of the seat itself was still letting off steam, and low flames flickered hopefully against the dark.

It felt like a lifetime had passed, but I knew it couldn't have been more than moments.

I tested out my arms, and though they protested heartily, they moved in the way I told them to.

I wanted to cry, but I was irrationally afraid that the tears would freeze on my face. Which made me realize I was thinking about a lot of irrational things. Like whether or not I'd be able to find my suitcase. And how much of my hair had burned off. I reached up. It had reached halfway down my back that morning, and now it seemed to be at my chin in more than a few places.

Is this it? I wondered. *Is this the* real *life changing moment?*

The last thought made survival instinct kick in, and I sat up, then stood up. The movement felt good, even though I was aching. And once I'd reassured myself that the airplane seat was done exploding, I decided to check out the fire.

It wasn't going to last long.

The plastic fibres from the seat were more interested in melting than they were in burning, and the stuffing seemed to be erupting into quick, blue-tinged flames that disappeared after only a few seconds.

With shaking hands, I gathered as many bits of fabric as I could and piled them onto the smoldering cushion. They lit immediately, and I cheered just a bit as I warmed my numb fingers over the fire. But my relief was short-lived. The synthetic fibres burned quickly, and I was soon staring at pile of steaming ash.

I sat as close as I could and tried to control my shaking.

If I don't start moving, I'll freeze, I thought.

I did some stretches, trying to keep my blood flowing. My bruised body protested heartily. My sliced hand was throbbing angrily, and after a very short period of time, it was the only part of my body that had any warmth at all.

I drew my arms into my sweater and huddled down close to the very last vestiges of rapidly-cooling ash. I felt myself drift, and shook my head, trying to stay alert. I wracked my brain, urging myself to remember everything I had ever heard about surviving when lost.

Build a shelter out of tree branches.

Not helpful.

Stay in one spot.

Did that still apply in arctic temperatures after a plane crash?

I almost laughed.

The fire was completely out now, and the wind was picking up. It was so very hard to judge time. And when the snow quickly began to cover any evidence that there had even been a fire at all, I gave up trying to guess just how long I'd been outside.

I wondered how many more minutes I could survive in the sub-zero temperatures in a cardigan, blouse, and dress pants. Thirty? Less?

Walk, I told myself. *Try to find another survivor, or a bigger piece of the plane. Something to use as shelter.*

When I stood up again, I realized immediately that mobility was going to be a problem for two big reasons.

First, the initial adrenaline that had pumped through my body after the crash had completely worn off. I could feel a concentrated pain in my knee, and when I put my hands on top of it, the swelling was apparent, even through my pants. A bad sprain or some torn ligaments, maybe.

And my second problem was an even worse one. I was no longer wearing shoes. My heels were gone.

"Oh, God," I moaned.

Had I been wearing them when I'd been stumbling around, collecting bits of airplane seat?

And more importantly, how come I couldn't feel the icy ground underneath my feet?

Panic made my heart thud irregularly in my chest, and I took a few desperate steps away from the vanishing plane seat. A crunching noise from somewhere behind me made me spin around.

I squinted against the blinding snow. I couldn't see anything but white.

"Hello?" I called out hoarsely.

I spun around again, and I realized that I could no longer make out the spot where the airplane seat had been just seconds earlier.

I started to walk, spurred equally by the hope that someone was coming to my rescue, and by the fear that something might be chasing me.

My legs moved leadenly, and my sore knee slowed me down even more.

"Go, go, go!" I ordered out loud.

I tried to run, and immediately lost my footing.

Oh.

No.

I pitched forward, and found myself rolling, rolling, rolling, down a steep and bumpy hill. My skull cracked against something hard, and as my downward tumble continued, I told myself that I really had to stop banging my head on stuff.

***

I'd made things worse for myself. Much worse, in fact.

I was groggy, and my body was aching twice as bad. My knee throbbed, and the wrist I'd cut earlier felt like it was on fire.

I was lying on my side, and I could see the steep side of a rocky hill, dotted with ice and snow. It was a wonder that I was still alive, really, judging from the size of the cliff-like plunge I'd taken. At least the wind was no longer whipping directly into my face.

My brain struggled to make sense of my situation, but my thoughts were slippery, and somewhere in the back of my mind I knew that hypothermia must be setting in. I'd learned the symptoms from a nature show I'd watched earlier in the year. I listed them off, trying to at least put my circumstances into a tidy mental box.

Severe shivering.

Yes, I had that.

My teeth were chattering uncontrollably. So no doubt there.

Difficulty breathing.

I drew in some air, and my throat and lungs constricted. It could've been from the cold.

Or it could be psychological, I admitted.

"Probably both," I said out loud.

Irregular heartbeat.

Definitely.

It was thumping uncontrollably in my chest. Though maybe hypothermia would slow it down, eventually.

Yes, probably.

The thought was distracting, and I wondered if death like this would be painful.

Did this count as heading into an irrational state of mind? It was another symptom, I knew. If things followed the same course of events as they had in the nature program, I would start taking my clothes off soon. Paradoxical undressing, it was called.

"What a thing to remember," I muttered, and admitted that, yes, my words weren't entirely clear. "Well, if I'm going to die, I might as well go down kicking."

Definitely irrational, I acknowledged.

I struggled to sit up, and I couldn't. My hand was buried in the snow, and it was pinned down by something as well.

"Oh, crap," I croaked.

I flopped down onto the snow and winced as my already sore head bumped the ground.

"Wish I had a warmer blanket," I murmured.

I reached out and tried to grab an imaginary down comforter to pull up to my shaking jaw, then twitched back uncomfortably as I realized a dark, soulful eye, set in the side of a furry face, was staring eerily down at me.

"Hello there," I said as brightly as I could manage.

The reindeer tilted its head to the side, and made a small sound in the back of its throat.

"I'd shake your hand – err, hoof – but I'm quite stuck, you see," I explained helpfully.

I could hear my words slurring together.

The reindeer pawed the ground, then looked up suddenly, startled. His ears flattened nervously, and I closed my eyes. The snow felt oddly warm against my cheek, and I sighed gratefully before jerking my head back up again. I looked around. The reindeer was gone, and it made me unreasonably sad.

It was quiet, and I wanted to sleep.

The snow still fell, and I watched the flakes crystallize on my sweater.

Don't sleep! I shouted mentally, but it was useless.

The world was too dark, the snow was too pretty, and I was just too tired to keep holding on.

Chapter Three

My face burned, and I could hear someone screaming, high-pitched and incessant. I wanted it to stop. Desperately.

Dear Lord, I thought. *I'm making that noise.*

I tried to cut myself off mid-scream, but I couldn't. I hurt all over, but the pain in my feet was the unbearable kind. So I let myself yell, and yell, and yell.

Get away from it, I told myself. *Run.*

I attempted to move my legs away from the source of the burning pain. But I was unable to move.

I gritted my teeth and pulled as hard as I could. My legs wouldn't budge. Something was holding them in place. I tried to sit up and realized that my hands were bound as well. I writhed against the restraints and started to scream again, this time as much in fear as in pain.

Hands landed on my shoulders, pushing me down, and then someone was trying to force my eyes open with cool-tipped fingers. I shook my head violently against the intrusion, and the onslaught stopped immediately.

I heard some shuffling, and someone touched my burning feet. I shrieked loudly before I realized that whatever was being done was cooling the horrible heat and soothing the pain away into something tolerable. A warm and comforting cloth landed on my forehead. I took a deep breath, stopped fighting, and opened my eyes.

I was lying flat, staring up at a tent-like ceiling, no more than three feet from my face. A warm, orange light made shadows dance across the surface.

Where am I?

A wrinkled face in a fur-lined leather hood leaned over me, and I cringed back, startled. The face smiled, exposing a nearly toothless mouth.

She said something to me in a gruff but feminine voice. It sounded like gibberish.

"I need a hospital," I tried to tell her, but it came out as a raspy whisper.

The old woman's smile turned into a grin, and I wondered if she was senile, or if she just didn't speak English.

"Hos-pi-tal," I repeated slowly.

The word burned against my throat.

The woman frowned and leaned closer to my face. She smelled like wood-smoke and leather. She spoke again, and I still couldn't understand her. The language sounded vaguely Slavic, but it was a totally unfamiliar dialect.

I shook my head to show her that I didn't understand. She pulled away, squatting on her heels beside me. Her head didn't even brush the roof, and I decided that she must be tiny. She pursed her lips thoughtfully, then shouted something. It was another word I didn't recognize. But clearly it was important to her. She repeated it over and over.

"Gavril!"

Once. Twice. And a third time so loudly that I wanted to cover my ears.

A vibration under my back stopped. I hadn't even really been aware of the sensation until it ceased.

We were moving, I realized.

A blast of cold air swept across my body momentarily, and I felt immediate panic. I started shivering again, and the old woman said something in an angry voice.

The cold air cut off instantly, and a large, masculine form crawled in to crouch down beside the woman. His head punched at the ceiling, making it billow upward.

He growled something at the woman, and she shook her head.

I tried helplessly to follow the exchange between the two, but of course it made no sense to me.

Not yet.

But I had no intention of sticking around long enough to learn their language.

Hospital. Then home.

After a few more heated words from the woman, the man raised his hands in a helpless gesture and shuffled over to me.

I watched him warily, very conscious of his size. Even crouched as low he was, his head continued to press against the tent-like roof. And his shoulders were broad enough to block out anything else.

He was dressed in fur, just as the woman was, but his ensemble included a frightening face mask. It was like the leather version of a balaclava. His eyes – dark and intelligent – stared at me from behind it. Disdainfully. Irritably. I knew immediately that *he* had tied me down like this. And it made me mad.

He said something. Slowly. Like he was talking to a small child. Or a very stupid adult.

Which made me even angrier.

I pretended that I couldn't hear him.

He sighed and turned toward the woman.

They argued for another few moments, and she poked him in the chest, hard.

He turned his attention back to me.

"Hoos-ba-tull," said the old woman, mimicking my earlier enunciation.

The man grunted and looked at me for confirmation.

"Hospital," I whispered.

His eyes widened as if he was surprised that I could talk at all. He fired off a series of questions and waited for my response.

I tried to shrug my shoulders, but the restraints prevented it, so I just gave him a blank stare.

He growled something that I took to be a curse.

I still said nothing. The pain in my feet was returning, and I could feel sweat breaking out on my forehead underneath the cloth. I shivered before I could stop myself.

For one moment, I thought I saw concern play through the man's eyes, but it was gone so quickly that I might have imagined it. He turned and murmured something to the old woman. When he faced me again, there was no hint of compassion there.

He tapped his chest lightly.

"Gavril," he said.

"Whatever," I replied.

It was rude and I knew it, but my feet were really starting to burn again, and the throb in my knee reminded me that I'd injured that, too. My throat was raw, I couldn't feel my hands at all, and I didn't like being tied up. I really wasn't in the mood for playing name games.

"Gavril," he repeated impatiently.

The old woman pushed him aside and pointed to herself.

"Lanka," she told me, then put her hand on the man's arm and nodded her head toward him. "Gavril."

"Yeah, I get it," I said.

The woman waited expectantly.

"You Tarzan, me Jane," I muttered.

"Lanka," she repeated. "Gavril."

"Lanka," I conceded with a sigh.

I refused to look at the man named Gavril.

Lanka tapped *my* chest.

"Lindsay," I said.

"Lin-zee." Lanka sounded pleased.

Gavril spoke to her irritably, and she gave him a doubtful look. But when he repeated himself, Lanka turned around to fiddle with something at the edge of the tent.

I avoided looking at Gavril and focused my attention on watching Lanka instead. She was engrossed in whatever she was doing, and was talking to herself out loud.

I could feel Gavril staring at me, and I made the mistake of glancing at him in return. His eyes were burning with anger and I was irrationally annoyed that he wouldn't take his mask off.

What are you hiding? I wondered.

"Gavril," he growled when I met his gaze.

"I heard you the first ten times," I croaked.

He asked me a question. I shook my head vehemently, not really caring what he wanted to know. He asked again, and I looked the other way.

So he reached down and squeezed one of my feet.

The pain was excruciating. I shrieked and thrashed against my bonds.

Lanka spun around, caught Gavril's smug look, and slapped him across the face.

Ha. Take that.

He hung his head apologetically and started to back away. He kept going until I could only see his covered face. He glanced at me one more time, and I saw a surprising amount regret in his eyes before he was gone.

Jerk.

Cold air passed through the tent, and in a moment Lanka was by my side, tipping a warm beverage down my throat as she murmured soothing-sounding words. I swallowed the liquid gratefully. It felt good against my sore throat.

"Thank you, Lanka," I said sincerely.

She smiled and stroked my hair. The pain in my feet – even the one that Gavril had squeezed – subsided, and I started to feel sleepy. I closed my eyes, enjoying the warmth that engulfed me. I thought I heard a man's voice shouting something from outside, and then the hum of movement resumed under my back.

If an ambulance came as a sled, I thought sleepily. *This might be it.*

I worked to stay conscious, but I couldn't fight it for long, and after just a few minutes, my exhaustion won out.

***

I opened my eyes.

I felt triumphant at first, then disturbed.

The scenery was all wrong.

Reality hit me, and it was accompanied by a terrible smell. Rusty and dirty. I tried to breathe through my mouth to avoid it, and I gagged on the thickness of the air.

I didn't know where I was, but it wasn't the moving tent – the sled-slash-ambulance. It was bigger, and browner, and loud with the sound of voices arguing in a foreign language.

I saw Lanka. Or I thought I did.

My head spun, and when I tried to catch another glimpse of her, I became dizzy. I tipped my head sideways just in time to throw up. Someone wiped my chin.

I was still tied down, at least by my legs, which immediately made me look around for Gavril. It both annoyed me and filled me with relief when I didn't spot him.

Someone shoved something hard and flat into my mouth and held it there. I tried unsuccessfully to spit it out.

I caught a flash of something else – shiny, but not metallic – and it terrified me. Agony, sharp and long shot up my right hand and through my arm. I regretted having thought my feet hurt before. Compared to this torment, my feet felt nothing.

It went on indefinitely. I bit down on the object in my mouth, understanding that it was there to counter the pain, and to stop me from biting off my own tongue.

When I said hospital, this wasn't what I meant.

Lanka came to my side, and this time I knew it was her for sure. Her face was sympathetic and she touched my forehead lightly.

Please, I begged mentally. *Make it stop.*

And finally it did lessen.

Lanka pulled the unnamed thing out of my mouth and tipped a wooden cup to my lips. I drank. I threw up again, then drank some more.

I slept for hours. Or days. I couldn't tell. My consciousness was alarmingly irregular, and when I was awake, the pain was mind boggling. I stopped trying to figure out where I was, or why. I was just too weak to keep doing it.

I kept hoping to open my eyes and see the white, sanitary wall of a proper medical facility. For the medicinal scent of bleach to fill my nose.

All I got was Lanka. She spoon fed me a tangy soup, alternated pouring cold and warm water down my throat, and changed my bedding with humiliating frequency. I gave up being embarrassed quickly, and resigned myself to my temporarily invalid state.

I dreamed often and I dreamed vividly, sometimes of Ben, but mostly of Anna and the two women whose Russian names were slipping away from me already. Had they made it out alive? I found it unlikely. Even the miracle of my own survival didn't give me much hope. And that made my heart ache.

Sadie flitted in and out of my thoughts too, and I wondered if news of the crash had reached home. Would I be presumed dead? Would the search for my body have started already?

But of all my visions, the most vivid were the ones of the masked man and the malice he spat my way. I saw his mostly-hidden visage, over and over. I felt his hands, tying me up, or squeezing my toe.

Why did he hate me? I would wonder each time his face floated to mind, and always following that, *Why did he save me?*

And each time I woke, it was in a cloud of regret, and loss, and that was almost worse than dreaming.

Lanka was my only anchor in the world, stroking my face and feeding me more hot liquid and murmuring incomprehensible things.

I'm going to die here, I concluded as I fought to stay awake another time and failed. *Next to a man who prefers me tied up, and under the care of an old woman with no teeth.*

***

I gasped out loud as true consciousness hit me suddenly.

Warm water caressed my skin, and I leaned into the pleasant sensation with a sigh. I thought I felt something moving along my back, applying pressure as the water hit me. I relaxed into the pleasurable feeling. It felt good on my aching muscles. And it was so much better than... Better than what?

I froze, fear and panic replacing pleasure, and my eyes flew open.

I swore, loudly and emphatically.

Hazy memories of the last few days tumbled around in my brain.

The crash. The snow. My fitful sleeping and waking pattern, fuelled by the icy weather and my injured state. I shook my head, trying to focus on the present.

I was propped up in a fairly deep, in-ground tub. My legs and torso were fully submerged, and warm water lapped at my armpits. My arms were held up at shoulder level, and strapped securely to two wooden posts. My right hand had been wrapped in thick linen-like bandages that came up nearly to my elbow, and the whole thing throbbed quite thoroughly.

"Dammit," I muttered, and tried to free my arms.

I was getting very tired of being restrained.

Then a flurry of ripples in the tub beside me confirmed the fact that I wasn't alone.

A woman – older than Lanka even – glided from somewhere behind me to a spot just in front of me. She grinned, seemingly unaware of her own nudity, and uncaring of mine.

She had a thick cloth, made of the same material as my bandages, in her hand. She held the cloth up and squeezed it out over my shoulders, being careful to stop any of the water from hitting my hands. She made a simulated washing motion over her chest and looked at me quizzically. Then she held up the cloth and raised a nearly non-existent eyebrow in a questioning manner.

Was she asking my permission to wash me?

I almost laughed.

I'd been tied down at least twice, stripped, and tossed into some kind of bathtub, and *now* she wanted my permission.

"No, thank you," I told her with a head shake.

She shrugged, positioned herself beside me, and snapped her fingers above her head.

Two young women appeared at the side of the tub. I watched them curiously. They wore identical outfits – tan tunics and matching pants, decorated with just a few bits of brown embroidery. They stared back at me, fear clear in their eyes. I tried to smile at them. They stepped a little closer to each other, whispering.

My companion in the tub rolled her eyes and snapped her fingers again.

The two girls jumped. One bent down to help the old woman climb out, while the other procured a woven towel from somewhere. Once the woman was out and wrapped in the towel, they all stepped away from the tub and out of my line of vision. I could hear the girls talking for a few moments, and then there was silence.

I sighed.

I had no idea where I was, how long I'd been there, or how I was going to get home. I was sore. I was scared. I was tired.

I closed my eyes, wishing that I had a wall to bang my head against.

"Lin-zee," said a deep voice from somewhere above me.

I looked up and almost jumped out of my skin. Dark eyes met mine.

Gavril.

I screamed, long and loud, and yanked on my arms, trying to free them from their bonds.

He reached into the tub and covered my mouth with a gloved hand. It was icy and covered in melting snow. The bits of fur on his mitt tickled the inside of my mouth, and I choked and gagged in response.

He let go slowly, but the look in his eyes let me know that he was ready to do the same thing again if I so much as squeaked.

Dear God, what does he want? I wondered.

I stared at him silently, desperately wishing that my arms were free so I could cover myself up.

Gavril gazed back at me. He still wore the leather mask, and his eyes were cold and emotionless. I stared back.

No. Not emotionless, I corrected. *Just perfectly controlled.*

And if he cared at all that I was naked, he didn't show it.

"What?" I whispered.

He said nothing, but finally flicked his hood off and drew the mask down around his neck. His hair was as dark as his eyes, and stubble covered his cheeks. His face the very definition of ruggedly handsome. Breath-catchingly so. I had to admit it, even if I didn't want to.

His strong, well-defined jaw was set in a stiff line, betraying the only hint at his true mood.

He'd taken off the physical mask. But it was obvious to me that he was still wearing a metaphorical one.

I made myself keep my eyes level with his, willing him to keep his distance. Instead, he stepped closer, crouching down by the tub. I took a breath, preparing to scream again. I decided that it was worth the risk of getting a mouthful of fur-lined glove. I tipped my chin up defiantly, ready to receive an angry hand against my lips.

But something else passed across Gavril's face.

What was it? Amusement? What was funny?

For just a second, flecks of gold danced across his eyes, and a tiny smile touched the corners of his mouth. I thought for a minute that if he really did smile, he'd probably knock those good looks of his straight out the park.

Then the tiny glimpse of a grin was gone.

He said something I couldn't understand, drew up his mask and hood, and stalked away.

I stared after him angrily. I was more furious that he had walked out on me than I was at his initial intrusion. I muttered aloud to myself, trying to sort through the jumble of emotions I was feeling.

"How dare he come in here and…And do what? Look at me? Look at me naked? He didn't even seem to notice."

There was something about the man that unnerved me. And infuriated me. I didn't like it.

Before I could delve into my thoughts any further, the two young girls reappeared at the side of the tub, looking even more nervous than before.

"Yes?" I snapped.

One of them jumped back, bumping into someone else. *Lanka.* I was almost relieved to see her. At least she was a familiar face. And at least she wasn't Gavril.

"Lin-zee?" she said, completely ignoring the two girls.

"Lanka, good to see you."

I sounded like I was greeting her in a coffee shop line up.

What I wouldn't give for a latte and scone, I thought, and my stomach growled.

Lanka smiled. She said something slowly and looked at me hopefully.

I shook my head.

Sorry, lady. Even I'm not that good.

She shrugged and knelt down beside the tub, then put a palm out and used two fingers on her other hand to make a scissoring motion across the surface.

"What? Charades?" I asked.

Lanka repeated the gesture and looked at me with inquisitive patience. She made the motion a third time, and I finally got it.

I shook my head again. "Doubtful."

Lanka looked so disappointed that I felt bad.

"It's not that I don't *want* to walk. It's just that don't know if I *can*," I apologized.

She smiled encouragingly and said something I was sure meant *please.*

"I guess I could try," I told her.

I actually had no idea what kind of shape I was in. I looked down at my knee, remembering the swelling I had seen there before. It did look better. A lot better. I nodded at Lanka, and she grinned.

She snapped her fingers, and the two girls – who had been watching with silent interest – scrambled to bring another woven towel to the tub. They reached down and undid my arms, being careful not to get any water on my bandaged hand. When they were done, I stood up on shaky legs and smiled at them.

"Can you help me out, too?" I asked, pointing to the ground beside the tub.

They seemed to understand, and grabbed me gently, then held me steady while I climbed out.

"Thank you," I said.

Lanka watched impassively as I towelled off. When I was done, the two girls started handing me articles of clothing. They gave me my own underwear first, and I was so pleased to see them that I had to fight back tears. Everything else was unfamiliar. I put on a tunic that was essentially the same as theirs and Lanka's, then slipped into a pair of fur-lined pants as well.

I was breathing hard by the time I was done, and I had to lean against one of the younger women, a bit embarrassed by my fragility. While I tried to catch my breath, I looked around the room.

It was quite a large building, really, with four tubs that could probably comfortably fit five people each. A pit, full of steaming rocks, was in the centre of the room, and some squat-looking benches lined the perimeter. The walls were made of dried mud. A stack of wooden buckets rested at the bottom of a mildly sloped ramp. The whole room was lit from above, and though I couldn't actually see the source of the light, I assumed that it must be some kind of oil-lamp system. The set-up made me think of a crudely fashioned spa.

I inhaled, eased myself off the girl I was leaning on, and gave her arm a grateful squeeze.

Lanka tapped me on the shoulder, then gave me a thick parka and a pair of leather boots. She put on a coat, too, and reached into the pockets to grab a pair of mittens. She pointed to my pockets, and I found another pair in there. I struggled to get one onto my good hand, but there was no way my bandaged hand was going to fit into the other one.

I held up the hand and shrugged. Lanka copied the gesture with a smile. She took a piece of leather cord and tied it around my waist, then around her wrist.

"Okay," I said.

She led me up the ramp to a buttoned leather flap where she unhooked a long strip of carved-bone buttons and pulled me into an enclosure that was barely big enough for the two of us. The air was colder in the little room, and it became quite dark as Lanka refastened the buttons from the inside. She did it quickly, and then turned to face a second flap. This one was fur-lined, and looked heavier than the first one, but it was done up with the same kind of buttons. Lanka opened those, too, and the flap swung open.

Icy air hit my face, and I buried my nose in my parka as the wind cut away my breath. In spite of my warm clothing, I shivered.

Lanka secured the outdoor flap, then began to walk across the snow-covered ground. She took quick steps, and I followed her because I had to. My legs ached, and I knew that I was shaking uncontrollably underneath my fur. I stumbled more than a bit, and I couldn't help but wonder how Lanka knew which direction was the right one.

I lifted my head briefly, trying to puzzle it out, but all I could see were white ridges and embankments against a backdrop of snowstorm.

When Lanka stopped abruptly, I sagged against her in relief.

"Dear God, where am I?" I tried to say, but the wind whipped away the words.

Lanka turned her body toward me slightly and placed an arm around my waist. I leaned on her, feeling guilty for relying on this older woman for support. She started moving again, this time more slowly, and I knew it was for my benefit.

I kept my face down and let her lead me. I was sure we walked for two minutes or less, but it seemed to take forever. Every step made me ache. Every inch made me gasp for air that I couldn't suck back quick enough.

We stopped at last, and Lanka disentangled herself from me. I felt instantly exposed. Even terrified. I dared to glance up, squinting against the blinding whiteness. Another tent flap loomed in front of us, and Lanka reached out confidently and began to unfasten the buttons.

I watched her, wondering why anyone would choose to live like this. And then I felt bad. I should've been nothing but thankful. If Lanka and her companions hadn't chosen to live this way, I'd already be dead, I could admit that. But even if it hadn't been for the isolation from modern day amenities, it still would have seemed like such a cold and hopeless place. Truthfully, I couldn't wait until I could figure out how to get myself back to civilization.

Lanka shuffled me into the now open flap and freed herself from the cord attaching us together before sealing the tent again. She pushed her hood down and grinned at me. I smiled back, and she pointed at the other flap, the one leading inside.

"Me?" I asked, surprised.

"Lin-zee," she agreed.

I fumbled with my one mitten, finally pulling it off with my teeth before shoving it ruefully in my pocket. I eyed the bone buttons a little nervously. My other hand was starting to throb again, and I didn't think it was going to be much help in the endeavour.

"I suppose I shouldn't use my teeth for *this*," I muttered.

Lanka just continued to smile. She waved toward the interior flap again. I reached up and started with the top button. And by the time I got to the third one, at chest level, I was panting.

Lanka placed a hand gently on my arm. I turned to look at her, shaking. She nodded with satisfaction, then pushed me out of her way.

As she swiftly undid the rest of the buttons, it occurred to me that Lanka had just given me some sort of test. I only had a second to wonder if I'd passed before she ushered me inside.

A hundred scents and sights greeted me. Assaulted my senses. I blinked, trying to sort out my new environment. It was warm – almost too much so – so I didn't protest as Lanka pulled my coat off. She showed me to a wall lined with pegs, and helped me hang the parka up beside several others that were just like it.

Wherever we were, it smelled delicious. Spicy and sweet at the same time. My mouth watered involuntarily. I wondered how long it had been since I'd eaten anything but the lukewarm broth Lanka had been feeding me while I'd been immobilized.

My eyes were starting to adjust, too.

This is a house, I realized.

Past the coat pegs, the walls were covered with overlapping fabric panels.

I could see a table, low-to-the-ground and surrounded by pillows. It wasn't made of wood – it actually looked more like paper mache than anything else. It was wide and long.

Something bubbled over top a cook fire, and it was clearly the source of the enticing aroma. I pushed down an urge to go over and peek inside.

"Oh!" I exclaimed, startled to realize that Lanka and I weren't alone.

A little boy and an obviously pregnant woman stood beside the food, and they were staring at me with undisguised curiosity.

"Hello," I said.

Immediately after I spoke, the boy ducked behind his mother.

"Hello," I said again and bent down to his level.

I heard the boy giggle, and he edged out and grinned at me.

Lanka pointed to the table, and the boy grabbed my good hand and pulled me to it. I joined him without arguing, sitting on a pillow that was definitely too small for my rear end.

I heard a gruff snort, and when I looked up, I saw that Gavril had joined the party. Grim amusement crossed his features as he took in the view of me balancing on the tiny pillow. I narrowed my eyes at his obvious entertainment at my expense, but he turned away when he saw me watching him, and seated himself at the head of the table. As far away from me as possible. After a moment, Lanka joined him, and he wiped all expression from his face.

I felt a tug on my borrowed shirt.

The little boy who'd brought me to the table was looking up at me. He asked me a question in his own language, and I shook my head.

But the boy didn't give up. He pointed emphatically at the empty cushions at our table and said something. I shrugged, and he sighed dramatically.

The pregnant woman, who I guessed to be about my age, began handing out clay bowls full of steaming stew. She smiled at me as she placed one in front of me, and patted my shoulder reassuringly.

Gavril snapped something at her, and she gave him a nervous glance before retrieving a tray of roundish buns and setting them in the centre of the table. As soon as everyone was served, she sat down across from me.

I watched everyone help themselves. They scooped the stew up with the buns, and after a moment, I followed suit, digging in awkwardly with my un-bandaged left hand.

My other arm was really starting to hurt, but the hunger I felt was outweighing even that.

And the food tasted as good as it smelled. It had a fish base, and it was full of rooty vegetables. I finished it in minutes, and the pregnant woman refilled my bowl automatically. I did my best to eat the second helping more slowly.

"This is delicious," I said out loud to no one in particular.

The little boy smiled, and I decided that I liked him. I pointed at my chest and said my name until he repeated it. Then I pointed at his chest, and he giggled.

"Andrik," he told me.

His face lit up suddenly, and he started pointing at things all over the room. Pretty soon I could say bowl and stew and table and chair and quite a few other words.

"You're pretty clever, aren't you Andrik?" I said, and tapped his head. "Smart."

He frowned for second, then tapped *my* head.

"Lin-zee, smart," he told me in English.

"This is definitely the beginning of a beautiful friendship," I agreed.

And that was when I realized that everyone in the room was staring at us. Andrik noticed, too.

"Lanka," he told me, and then added, "Gavril. Nanaj."

"Hi, Nanaj," I said to the pregnant woman.

Lanka looked pleased, and the pregnant woman seemed impressed, too. Only Gavril's face was full of irritation. When he saw me looking, he snapped something at Nanaj again. She was just filling up his bowl, and as a result of Gavril's sudden outburst, Nanaj spilled a bunch of soup in Lanka's lap. Gavril grabbed Nanaj's arm roughly and growled something at her.

"Hey!" I shouted automatically.

Gavril turned his angry gaze toward me.

I shot him a returning look, just as furious. "Don't even bother directing that garbage my way. You'll pull back a stump instead of a hand."

Nanaj retrieved a woven cloth from somewhere and began to wipe up the mess.

"*You* should be doing that," I muttered in Gavril's direction.

Nanaj frowned at both of us, and looked at Lanka. The older woman rolled her eyes, then spoke sharply to Gavril. As she chastised him emphatically, his face went hard. He jumped up, grabbed the cloth, wiped up the spilled soup, and left the table in a hurry, very nearly shoving Nanaj as he went by.

I looked down at my bowl, feeling like an intruder.

Lanka said something softly to Nanaj, and the pregnant woman sat down. I met her eyes, and realized that she was on the verge of tears. My irritation at Gavril spiked again. I wished I had the words to tell Nanaj it wasn't her fault. But she shook her head ever so slightly, then took a very deliberate bite of her bun. After another moment, we all went back to eating, and even Andrik went silent.

When we were done and Nanaj had cleared away our bowls, Andrik helped me up and gestured for me to follow him.

"Come," he said, and I understood him.

I smiled slightly, pleased with myself.

He held my good hand tightly and pulled me through a cavernous hallway.

We stopped in front of a set of fur drapes, and Andrik pulled them aside. I peeked inside and saw a wide sleeping palette propped up on wicker-looking legs. Aside from a big, flat rock in the corner of the room, there were no decorations or other adornments.

Andrik pointed at himself and then at the bed.

"Nanaj and Andrik," he told me.

I nodded my understanding, and he led back into the hall. He paused briefly in front of a wide, beautifully beaded drape.

"Gavril," he whispered.

"Right," I muttered. "His highness would need his own room."

Andrik put his hand over his mouth, then shook his head.

"Sorry," I whispered.

He grabbed my hand and pulled me along a few more feet. We stopped in front of a second set of fur drapes, this one much narrower than the first, and Andrik let me lift them open myself. It was a small sleeping area made up of a pile of fur blankets.

"Lin-zee," Andrik said.

"I'm not going to sleep just yet," I told him in English.

But before I could even finish my protest a huge yawn overtook me, and Andrik giggled. I wasn't just sleepy, I was completely exhausted.

The excitement of food, of being in a new environment, and of being away from the frightening room where I had earlier experienced so much pain – *how long ago was that, anyway?* – had temporarily pushed aside that exhaustion. But now that I was full, clean, and warm, it hit me again with full force.

Lanka came up behind us and shooed Andrik away. She smiled at me and patted my hand.

"Smart," she said in English, pointing to her head.

"Yeah," I agreed sleepily.

Lanka half-pushed me onto the sleeping pad, and I had to cover another big yawn. She nodded with satisfaction, patted my hand again, and closed the curtains on her way out.

"Okay," I murmured, and covered myself with a fur blanket. "Just this once. But tomorrow, we get down to the getting-me-home business."

It occurred to me suddenly that if the roles had been reversed – if Lanka had shown up, lost, broken and unable to speak my language – I'd be calling the police. Or Social Services. Or both.

As I started to drift off, full of warm stew, and more comfortable than I would've been on my pillow-top mattress at home, I heard Gavril speak through my curtains. His voice was hushed, but angry.

For a split second, I sympathized. I was a stranger in this house. An invader.

Is it his house? I wondered.

I thought that it had to be.

And yes. If the roles really were reversed, I'd have been worried, too.

But then I remembered the shove he'd given Nanaj, and my heart hardened again before I drifted off to sleep.

***

I woke up screaming.

The pain in my hand was terrible beyond words. Worse than my feet had felt after Gavril and Lanka had rescued me.

I pushed my blankets aside frantically, searching for an outlet I couldn't possibly find.

"No!" I shouted.

A cool hand met my forehead, smoothing back my hair. Instinctively, I tried to bite it as it went past my mouth. The hand drew back with a startled intake of breath. It came back again, hesitant this time, and I gnashed at it again.

I'm sorry, I wanted to say. *I don't seem to be able to help myself.*

Someone said something sharply in a foreign language, and memory kicked in.

Lanka.

I tried to sit up. Rough hands grabbed my shoulders, pushing me back down.

"Stop," I gasped, but I wasn't strong enough to fight back.

I let my body go limp, trying to make sense of my suffering. I had felt fine at mealtime. What was different now?

Searing pain shot from my bandaged hand and up through my arm. It ached. It throbbed. It pierced.

I screamed again, letting it out.

"Lin-zee."

The voice was deep and soothing, and I made myself look for the source.

"Lin-zee."

It was something to focus on, to distract me from my agony.

Brown eyes, flecked with gold, were inches from my own. And brown hair, soft and not-quite straight, brushed my cheek.

Gavril.

What was he doing in my bedroom?

It's his bedroom, I reminded myself. *But still...*

His steady gaze held mine, though, and when he spoke, his breath danced not unpleasantly across my mouth.

"Lin-zee. Cup," he said.

I recognized the word from Andrik's word game at the table.

Oh, I thought. *Yes.*

Lanka had been feeding me something from a cup every few hours for the entire time I'd been there. For how long? I still didn't really know. Two days? Three? More? It must've been some kind of homeopathic pain medication. But she hadn't given me any since... When? Before my bath, anyway.

I wondered if she'd withheld it on purpose, maybe to assess my pain management. If so, I'd probably failed her. Big time.

"Cup," Gavril repeated, a little more firmly.

I nodded, but he still held me tightly. I didn't bother to fight his grip.

Lanka appeared at Gavril's side. She had a clay cup in her hand and she eyed Gavril questioningly. He pulled me gently to a sitting position. He kept a stiff arm around my shoulders, and I tried not to notice how natural it felt to sink into him.

He nodded at Lanka.

She tipped the cup up, and I drank from it gratefully.

The relief came quickly. The pain in my hand and arm subsided to an ache, and warmth spread through my body. I felt a bit dizzy, and I realized immediately why I was able to remember only bits and pieces from the last few days.

You've been as high as a kite.

I handed the cup back to Lanka, leaving about half of the liquid inside.

"Don't want to be a junkie," I murmured.

Lanka looked pleased.

"Sorry for trying to bite you," I added.

I mimicked the motion to show her what I meant, and to my surprise, Gavril burst out laughing. The rich, pleasant sound was right beside my ear and for some unfathomable reason, it made me tingle a little. Startled by the reaction, I turned to look at him. Our faces were only inches apart again. And he stopped chuckling abruptly.

"Never mind," I muttered. "I wasn't trying to entertain you, anyway."

Lanka said something to Gavril, and he released me back into a prone position. I wanted to argue, but Lanka's potion was getting to me. She pulled the blankets up around my chin, and I sighed in defeat.

Gavril asked her a question, and she shook her head vehemently. He repeated himself, sounding irritated, and Lanka continued to shake her head. Gavril met my eyes, and for some reason, I knew that he had been offering to tie me up. Again.

You just try it, I thought sleepily. *See what happens.*

I felt a hand, warm and rough, graze my cheek right before I drifted off once again. And I was sure it was his.

Chapter Four

I stretched out against my blankets with a wide yawn. I'd been lying there for two days, and I was starting to feel lazy. I felt a little bit guilty, too, for enjoying the fur so heartily. It went against all my beliefs about conservation and animal cruelty. But it really was comfortable.

My hand started to throb again, and I knew that it was going to get worse before it got better.

I gritted my teeth in irritation. I was going to have to learn to live with the pain. I'd been taking up space in Gavril's house for too long.

I didn't know what Lanka had been giving me, but whatever it was, there was no way I could function normally while taking it. And if I couldn't function normally, there was no way I was going to learn to communicate properly with Lanka and her family. I needed to be able to talk to them if I wanted to figure out where I was. And how to get home.

Since I had no details about the crash, I had no idea if a search was underway, or if it *had* been underway, if I should expect help, or if I was on my own. With a tiny plane like the one I was on, and in a remote area like this, I thought anything might be possible.

I wondered if they had a phone hidden somewhere, or if they knew where the closest urban centre might be.

I forced myself to sit up. It was dark in my little room – almost pitch black. But my eyes adjusted quickly, and in a second, I spied a cup beside my bed.

I picked it up and sniffed it. It didn't have the same sweet smell as Lanka's concoction, so I took a hesitant sip. It tasted like mint-flavoured water. I took another big swallow, and I felt oddly invigorated.

I gulped down the rest. I rolled my eyes at the cup.

"Great," I said out loud to the empty room. "First downers, now uppers."

But it felt good to be clear-headed. I tossed the rest of the blankets off and stood up. I used the chamber pot, praying all the while that no one would come in. The previous afternoon, Andrik had walked in on me, and in spite of his giggles, I'd been thoroughly embarrassed. I ran my tongue over my teeth, and wished that I had my brush and paste with me. I smiled a little at that. It was definitely the least of my worries.

I eased my way through the fur drapes and headed in what I hoped was the right direction. It was even darker in the narrow hall than I remembered. Anxiety overwhelmed me.

"Hello?" I called.

No one answered.

I paused to lean against the dirt wall, the severity of my situation weighing heavily upon me. I knew my solution to learn to communicate with Lanka was the only viable option. If any of them spoke something other than their own language, they hadn't indicated it. It was almost laughable. I'd come to Russia to immerse myself completely in another culture, and now that I was being forced to do just that, I wanted nothing more than to get out.

A small hand suddenly worked its way into my own.

I looked down.

Andrik's face, serious and concerned, peered up at me through the darkness.

"Lin-zee," he said. "Lanka?"

"Okay," I agreed.

"Okay," he repeated.

He led me through the hall to the eating area where Lanka was waiting. Andrik hugged me, then her, and went running out the tent flap.

As soon as he was gone, Lanka handed me a thick bun slathered with some kind of jam, and started talking to me, slowly. She'd obviously decided that I capable of learning.

She pointed to my arm as I chewed, and repeated herself several times.

"Arm," I stated in her language. "I get it. You know, if you'd stop drugging me, I'd learn faster."

Lanka nodded. She had no idea what I'd said, but she still looked pleased.

She kept going until I had the words for pain, hand, no, and yes.

Then she gestured toward my bandages.

"Oh," I said. "You want to look at my arm."

Lanka pointed at me.

"You want *me* to look at my arm?" I asked, pointing at myself as well.

"Yes," she replied.

"Sure. All right."

Lanka stood and left the room briefly. She came back with a leather cord, and swiftly tied my elbow to the table.

"Hey," I protested half-heartedly, but she kept going anyway.

As soon as she started to unwrap the bandages, the throbbing worsened. I tensed, realizing it was probably best that my arm was secured to the table.

Lanka offered me a cupful of her sweet, herbal remedy, but I shook my head and looked up at the ceiling instead. I concentrated on the thatched material there, trying to discern a pattern in its make-up. The pain increased again, and I made myself examine the general structure of the house.

I thought that we were at least partially underground. The walls were a dirt base, and it seemed that they might actually be a part of the ground itself. The front entryway, where Lanka and I had come in a couple of nights before, was solid mud. But the rest of the room was insulated and covered. Something that looked like thick stoneware piping, ran from the middle of the room to the wall, and up a chimney. The chimney met with a wide, steaming pit at the bottom.

I was thoroughly impressed, and was about to comment on it when Lanka grabbed my chin and forced my gaze down to my hand.

If I hadn't been attached to my arm, I would've recoiled from it in horror. I still slunk back as best I could, but Lanka wouldn't let me look away. When I started to close my eyes, she barked an order at me.

"Okay," I whispered.

I knew why she wanted me to look. I'd have to accept the damages if I wanted to move on.

I focused on my arm first. Clumsy, sinewy stitching held together a gash, six inches in length. It had to have been done in a hurry, and I knew I had to have fought back. I had a hazy memory of thrashing against several sets of firm hands.

I continued my examination. Just below the stitching, a narrow splint appeared to be glued to my skin. I flexed the muscle experimentally, and my arm screamed in protest.

I had a sudden vision of an icy hill, *kerthumping* underneath me as I rolled down, hands thrust in front of my body to break my repeated falls. And then a sharp, jarring pain had extended from my wrist to just below my elbow.

I didn't know too much about bones, but I was pretty sure I'd broken one. I wondered if the crude setting would cause permanent damage.

I moved my assessment down to my hand next, and again I shied away involuntarily from the destruction.

I was missing – my God, *missing* – the pinky and the ring finger completely. The skin was crispy where the amputation had occurred, and I realized that someone must have cauterized the wound. The middle finger ended in a stub at the first joint, and the flesh there had been burned as well.

I tried to drag a memory out to match up with what I saw.

Lanka and Gavril had found me... How long after I crashed?

In my mind, it seemed both long and short. I'd run. I'd been exposed to the cold. I'd fallen down the hill. My arm had been buried in the snow for a long time.

So cold, I had thought as it happened. *So why does it burn?*

Then there had been firelight. The smell of blood, the flash of something shiny. The burn. Gavril and Lanka arguing. It all blended together.

And the pain had already been so intense, so searing.

"Frostbite," I whispered, and at last Lanka let me look away from my hand.

I didn't want to mourn the loss of a measly two and half digits. But I was already forming a list of things I wouldn't be able to do with that hand.

I would probably never be able to open a jar of pickles on my own.

I would no longer be able to lift my pinky at a fancy tea party.

I couldn't flip someone the bird.

It was a silly list.

And none of it would matter if I couldn't get home, anyway. Because I somehow doubted that Lanka and her family had pickles.

The older woman was watching my face. I smiled at her, then started to cry. She wiped my tears away with her sleeve.

Then she said something to me firmly. Once. Twice. Three times. And I understood.

"You're alive."

"Yes," I agreed softly. "I am."

Lanka pulled a salve out from somewhere and began rubbing it into the burns. I winced at first, but whatever was in the jelly-like substance was quite literally numbing. She loaded it thickly onto the burned areas and smoothed a thin layer over top the stitched-up gash. When she was done, she wrapped the whole arm in fresh bandages. I was relieved to see the damage covered up.

Lanka offered me the sweet-smelling cup, and again I declined to take it. Now that I had seen the source of the pain, I wasn't ashamed of needing the relief. I knew I was going to give in again, but I wanted to remain alert, at least for a little while.

Lanka sat back, resting on her heels, and gave me a thoughtful look. I could tell that she was trying to decide what to do with me.

I pointed at the door.

She shook her head.

I pointed again, and Lanka sighed.

"Nanaj!" she called, and the pregnant woman appeared.

The two had a brief exchange that I didn't understand at all, and then Nanaj grinned at me. She pointed at the door, and I nodded eagerly.

We got bundled up in our parkas, boots, fur-lined pants, and mittens. I smiled at the ritual. It was a lot of work to do, just so that we could go outside. I hoped for both of our sakes that I was going to last longer than five minutes.

I let Nanaj guide me through the two sets of tent flaps, and braced myself for the cold air.

And it *was* cold. But it wasn't the same biting chill brought on by the blizzard that had been raging last time I was outside. A breeze, not quite strong enough to cut my breath away, teased fresh snow up along the ground. As I followed its airy dance across our path, I realized for the first time that we were in a village.

I almost gasped in surprise.

I'd been assuming that Lanka and her family lived at some kind of isolated outpost. I knew that there had to be more than one household because I'd seen the other three women at the bathhouse, but I hadn't anticipated anything like this.

It was dark out, as was to be expected for many months of the year on this side of the Arctic Circle, but the area was lit up brilliantly. Large, glowing oil lamps hung from posts every few feet. In the warmth of their light, I could also see how Lanka had been able to find her way from one structure to the other without issue. Long ropes led from each sunken-in doorway, and there were dozens and dozens of them.

There were people – mostly women and children – everywhere, all dressed up as Nanaj and I were.

I gaped. There was no other word for it.

Nanaj let me stand there for a minute, taking it in. She was probably able to sense my astonishment. Then she nudged me with a smile, and I followed her through the village.

A few people waved or called greetings to my hostess, and no one seemed surprised to see me. I assumed that news of my arrival must have gotten out.

We stopped often, sometimes outside people's homes, sometimes inside. I met a lot of women, young and old, and I quickly learned a few polite greetings. They patted Nanaj's stomach, and made me repeat their names.

"Darya."

"Lada."

"Janik."

Pretty soon the names and faces ran together.

Nanaj liked to chat, and she didn't seem to mind that I didn't really understand her. I got the feeling that she was glad to be out of the house, and when I thought of Gavril and his bad temper, I couldn't really blame her.

She walked me through the whole village, and even though I was starting to ache all over, I found that I was enjoying her company.

We finally reached the front of a big building, and I thought it might be the one where I'd had the bath before. Two women were standing in front of it, speaking in low voices, and when we came closer, they both went silent, staring at me.

I flushed. So far, I'd been met with nothing but friendliness and mild curiosity. This was something different. Not hostility, exactly. Maybe assessment. And scrutiny, definitely.

"Hi," I greeted them in their language. "Nice to meet you."

They didn't reply. One was a plump woman in a very dark parka. She narrowed her eyes suspiciously. The other – tall, thin, and wrapped in a blanket – muttered something that I didn't understand.

Nanaj frowned, but said nothing.

Then the tall one jumped toward me and grabbed my arm. My sore arm. She had a furious look on her face. I yelped in both pain and surprise, but she ignored it. She turned my wrist over and began tugging at my bandages.

"Stop," I gasped in English. "Please."

The plump woman came forward slowly, and put her hand on the angry woman's arm.

"Duscna," she said quietly. "No."

The other woman stopped pulling immediately, though she didn't let go and she didn't look happy about the interference.

"I am Jereni," the plump woman told me.

"I am Lindsay," I replied, doing my best to pronounce the words correctly.

"Hmph," said the thin woman named Duscna.

She finally released my arm, and it throbbed in response to the mistreatment.

"Hi," I said awkwardly.

Duscna and Jereni each asked Nanaj a question, and she shook her head.

My head had started to pound. I was suddenly very tired, and the pain in my arm was getting much worse.

"Nanaj," I whispered, searching for the right word before settling on the only one I could remember. "House?"

All three women turned to me, surprised.

"House?" I repeated.

Nanaj took one look at my face and nodded. When we got back to the house, I didn't argue as she handed me back to Lanka, who poured her potion smugly down my throat, then led me to my pile of fur blankets, where I collapsed gratefully.

Not my blankets, I thought belatedly. *Gavril's.*

Chapter Five

I dreamed of Anna three nights in a row. And each morning, I awoke with guilt wracking my body and a sick feeling in my gut.

I distracted myself by following Nanaj around, and I was grateful for her patience and her company. I got the feeling that she was showing me off a bit, but I didn't mind. I had tried to ask her about the two angry women at the bathhouse, and she had brushed me off, pretending not to understand any of what I said. I gave up and decided to learn as much as I could by absorbing what I saw.

People seemed happy to pay attention to me, and the more they talked to me, the better I understood the language. I forced myself to speak as much as possible, and to remember everything I could. I was getting better at filling in the blanks when I was listening to the others talk, and I could already form rudimentary sentences.

But it was exhausting for me. I continued to rise later than everyone else in the house, and I went to bed hours before they did, too.

They let me eat dinner alone, and I was glad that at least I didn't have to see Gavril's frowning face when I was spooning in stew, or chewing on dried fish.

I didn't take Lanka's potion during the day, but I was afraid to refuse it at night. I didn't want to risk the suffering I had experienced without it.

The pain was rarely less than tolerable, and I wondered how long it would take before I really started to heal.

My few stuttering questions about the crash had been met with confusion or blank stares. So far, I hadn't been able to discern a word for *plane*, and if anyone knew what had happened to mine, they weren't letting on.

I'd considered whether or not Gavril might be the person to ask. And promptly rejected the idea. No way was I approaching him deliberately.

On what I estimated to be my tenth or eleventh day of staying at the house, I found myself debating whether or not to unwrap my arm, when Lanka came in from outside with her eyes narrowed.

"What?" I asked guiltily.

"Today, you go with Andrik," she told me.

I was startled.

"What?" I said again.

She answered me slowly. "You. And. Andrik. Together."

The impish boy appeared at her side with an excited grin on his face.

"Okay?" he asked in English.

I had to laugh. He was excellent at parroting all of my slang.

"Okay," I agreed.

I was actually thrilled at the idea of spending the day with Andrik. He was easy to communicate with, and each moment I spent with him gave me a better grasp of his language. I could usually puzzle out his sentences. Plus, he picked up English words with remarkable ease, and I had already had to un-teach him a few swear words.

"Follow me," he instructed, and I obliged.

I had figured out that everyone in the village – each of the People, as they called themselves – fulfilled a role from the time they could walk. Even the smallest kids gathered snow in buckets, which they used for melting into water for household use, and left them outside the doorways. There was a job for everyone. There was cooking, and weaving, and even sanitation duties. I was actually kind of excited to be involved in something other than trying to learn their language.

"We are doing what today?" I asked as I followed Andrik through the village.

"What are we doing," he corrected.

"Sorry, Little Boss," I said in English.

He giggled and pointed at the empty leather bag he was carrying.

"Rocks."

"Rocks?"

Andrik nodded.

I shrugged. "Okay then."

We walked for what seemed like quite a long time, and though we could still see the lights from the village, darkness pressed in on the other side. I worried that we'd gone too far, and I was about to say something when Andrik stopped.

"Here," he told me.

Andrik pointed at a patch of snow, and I shrugged again. He grinned and pulled something that looked like a flattened wooden spoon out of his pocket, and started digging. I watched him for a few minutes.

"Aha!" he said triumphantly, and pulled an egg-sized stone out from under the snow.

"Good," I praised.

If I'd known how to say amazing, I would have, because as I followed Andrik around, he stopped in seemingly random spots, dug, and each time pulled out a similar stone.

"Rocks for what?" I asked.

"To get warm," he told me.

"Oh."

Andrik looked at me and sighed. He always seemed to be able to tell when I didn't understand.

"Fire gets the rocks hot. The rocks are in the house," he explained simply.

"Oh," I said again, this time actually understanding.

Each of the partly underground homes was equipped with two hearths. One for cooking, and one for heating. The second one was always filled with red hot rocks, so that even when no one was home to directly tend the fire, the house didn't lose heat. And every bedroom had one big stone each, pre-warmed before bed each night.

"You dig?" Andrik suggested.

I shook my head ruefully and held up my lame hand. It was actually hurting worse than usual, and in spite of enjoying my little friend's company, I was kind of wishing that Lanka had found an inside job for me.

"Lazy," Andrik teased.

It seemed to be the worst insult the People could think of.

"Ouch," I said in English and made a pained face.

Andrik paused to look at me carefully.

"You almost froze?" he asked.

"Yes."

"Why didn't you just make a small house? Or get behind a hill?" he asked, puzzled.

"I fell *down* a hill. Does that count?"

I grinned as Andrik laughed at my expense. Out here, sub-zero survival was probably a basic life skill.

"I can't do any of that stuff," I admitted.

"But it's easy."

"Not for me."

"Like this," Andrik said.

He dragged me along until we found a raised patch of snow. He hollowed it out with his hands and huddled down inside. I bent down, too.

"I don't fit," I told him.

"You make one for *your* body."

"What else?" I asked.

"Find the mountain," he said. "And get home."

"Oh."

Andrik rolled his eyes and turned his little shovel over so that the pointed end was face downward. He drew an elaborate picture in the packed snow, showing me the layout of the entire region. He did his best to explain it, as well.

There was a range of mountains on one side, and a sheer and icy cliff on the other. There was some kind of basin in the middle, and the People lived in between the basin and the mountains. Water surrounded the entire land mass.

"An island?" I asked.

Andrik frowned. "A what?"

"Water everywhere," I said, and then added in English. "You need a boat to get here."

"Water everywhere," he agreed. "But what is a *boat*?"

"Wood, tied together to make a house that floats on the water," I elaborated, half in English and half in his language.

Andrik's eyes widened. I knew wood was a scarcity to the People, and it probably seemed strange that someone would build a floating house out of such a precious commodity.

"Never mind," I said dismissively, and went back to examining his drawing.

He started digging again, talking as he moved from place to place.

"My mom likes you," he said.

"I like her."

"Good."

"She gets lonely sometimes," he confessed.

"What about your dad?"

I thought again of the angry cloud that seemed to be ever-present on Gavril's face.

"What about him?"

"I guess *he* doesn't like me," I said.

"I haven't asked," he replied.

I went back to examining Andrik's drawing, and something suddenly crossed my mind. He had clearly depicted the Village, and had drawn the whole terrain, sea-to-sea. But he hadn't indicated any other occupied areas. If the People had no boats, and there was no other populated areas on the island, how was I going to get back to the mainland?

"Andrik, does anybody *else* live on your land?" I asked.

He froze, mid-dig. He tilted his head sideways and stood up, staring intently toward the lights of the village.

"Done with rocks," Andrik informed me abruptly, turning his eyes toward home.

He took off eagerly over the snow, and I as I hurried after him, I realized that he hadn't answered my question.

***

Something was happening back in the village.

Everyone was outside, and no one was working.

"What is it?" I asked Andrik.

But the little boy's eyes were shining excitedly, and he didn't seem to have heard me.

I looked for another familiar face and couldn't find one. Everyone was jostling around, and no one stayed in the same spot for more than a second or two.

I finally spotted Nanaj, and I grabbed her before she could run off.

"Please," I said. "What's happening?"

"They're home!" she told me excitedly.

"Who?"

She pointed, and then she was gone.

I strained to see over the crowd of people. Most of them were grinning. Many of them – even the adults – were bouncing on the spot. I tried to see what they saw, but felt like I was staring at nothing. For one second, I thought I spotted a silhouette on the horizon, but I blinked and it was gone.

I sighed in frustration. Then I heard something. Distant singing. And laughter.

The sounds got closer, and pretty soon I could also hear heavy footfalls crunching against the snow.

A small child broke out of his mother's arms and went dashing in the direction of the noise.

"Brother!" Someone yelled, and the cry was followed by a series of excited greetings and shouts of people's names.

"Welcome!"

"Jarin!"

"Larek!"

"At last!"

The crowd surged forward, and was met by the oncoming group. Very quickly, the village was teeming with men. They kissed the women and hugged the children.

I caught sight of Andrik just as he rushed toward a very tall man. The man tossed aside his pack and his spear, and bent down to grab the little boy. He lifted Andrik with ease, and swung him around. The two of them seemed so filled with joy that I almost had to look away.

Tears formed in my eyes, and I wiped them off, embarrassed.

The man looked up then, and he met my gaze straight on.

Even with the distance between us, I could tell that he was room-commandingly handsome.

His face was hawk-like in both its appearance and its ferocious intensity. He was clean-shaven, narrow-lipped, and staring back at me with no shame.

And his eyes widened as he took in my face. His stare lingered on my hair, and I reached up to touch it self-consciously. Much of it had burned off with the flaming airplane chair, and Lanka had trimmed the rest to match that length. I knew that it was sticking out from my hood in a frizzy mess. Its natural blonde stood out in the Village, where everyone was dark-haired. But the novelty of it had worn off for most of the People already.

I tried to smooth it down a little, but there wasn't much use in trying.

Andrik caught my gaze and he wriggled down and then tried to pull the man toward me. The man bent down and whispered something to him, and they pushed through the crowd to reach me.

"This is my uncle," Andrik told me as they approached.

"Hello," I greeted, blushing a little.

Up close, he was even nicer to look at, with angular, or maybe even sharp features. His eyes were so dark that they were near to black. I wondered whose sibling he was. He definitely looked nothing like Gavril, and I didn't think he looked anything like Nanaj, either.

"I am Taras," he stated formally.

"Lindsay."

I blushed an even deeper red as he examined me, head to toe. Unexpectedly, he reached out to touch my cheek. "What's wrong with your face?" The question wasn't rude; it was filled with fascination.

And my skin grew hotter still, and I knew that I must be crimson all the way up to the roots of my hair.

Has he never seen someone blush before?

Andrik nudged his uncle.

"How did you come to the People?" Taras asked.

I opened my mouth and then closed it again. Oddly enough, it was the first time anyone had asked me the question directly. I had been working under the assumption that Lanka must have already spread the story of my origin quite thoroughly throughout the village.

"It doesn't matter," Taras said decisively. "Right now, we celebrate."

It had probably been building that way anyway, but to me, it seemed as though his words triggered the party. Large drums were brought out of hiding, and a bonfire was built at either end of the main path through the village. Soon, the smell of roasting meat – brought in by the hunters – was everywhere.

Taras gripped my good hand tightly and pulled me around, insisting that I taste some of each thing being cooked. He stopped to greet groups of people, drummed and sang when called upon. His voice was melodious, a lovely baritone, and it was obvious that he was well-liked.

It felt odd to be carted around by this strange man. But it was exhilarating, too.

Taras was infectiously enthusiastic, and people seemed thrilled to see him. They laughed and slapped his back and offered him food. If they thought it was strange that he was pulling me around behind him, they didn't say it.

Andrik joined us at random intervals, sometimes following his uncle for a few minutes, sometimes just coming in for a hug and then running off.

Taras continued to drag me from house to house, and when I was good and breathless, he stopped in front of a door that was twice as wide as any other. He put his hand over his mouth and made sure that I understood that I wasn't supposed to talk.

We went in quietly, and when he helped me out of my coat, his eyes widened slightly at the sight of my injured hand. He looked like he wanted to say something, but he remained silent.

The structure we entered was a large, open room, lit in the centre by a glowing lamp. It was so quiet that at first I thought we were alone, and my heart beat nervously at the idea. But as Taras led me across the room, I realized there were other people in the room. Their forms were indistinct in the odd light, and if they cared about our intrusion, they didn't show it. Taras pulled me down, and we sat cross-legged on the cool, dirt floor.

Someone coughed, and then there was a general shuffling, and I found myself wedged right between Taras and an elderly man. I was hyper-conscious of the way every few seconds Taras's knee brushed my thigh, and when he threaded his fingers through mine, I was sure my heart must be beating loud enough for the entire circle to hear it.

But I soon forgot about myself entirely.

"The hunt went well."

The deep voice came from everywhere and nowhere at once, and I realized that the room had been designed with acoustics in mind.

"We are thankful for the safe return of our men, and for their success."

The second voice was feminine, but carried equally well. I thought I recognized it as belonging to the angry woman who'd grabbed my sore arm a few days before.

"A story!"

The third voice was young, and greeted with indulgent laughter that reverberated pleasantly through the room.

"The People have lived in this snow-covered land since time began to unfold."

The words were louder than the rest because they were spoken right beside my ear.

Taras.

"Not that story," complained the young voice.

"Let me guess... You want one with heroes?" Taras teased.

"Yes! Tell Pala's tale!"

A collective sigh came from all around me, and then the female voice picked up.

I listened intently, trying to catch every nuance. I followed along as best I could, latching onto words I recognized, and filling in the blanks everywhere else.

"Before we lived peaceably in the way that we know now, our ancestors were at war with the land itself. They fought to tame the snow, to bend the ice to their will. And they lost as often as they won. It was a life that could not be sustained, and the People struggled to survive. Then Pala, son of Malek, son of Demi, was born. He was a brave man. A worthy man. By virtue of his birth, Pala ruled the people," she said. "And the People were pleased with his leadership for many years. But on the eve of his eighth season as ruler, the Freeze was a dangerously long and perilous one. The People began to starve. Food was scarce, and men feared leaving their homes. And so Pala set out to hunt, on his own, in the deadly cold, with nothing but his spear and his intuition. He was gone for many days, and the People feared the worst. His young wife, Ria, who was blind, but gifted with a second sight, assured the People that Pala would return. But Ria was also pregnant, and as the days dragged on, some began to suspect that her internal sight was clouded by the impending birth of the heir to Pala's throne. The tiny Village, then little more than icy huts, lay in wait. Soon, the People began to fight amongst themselves. Many of the men in the Village were killed in skirmishes, and among those was Pala's brother-in-law, who was meant to be caring for Ria."

She paused, and I found that I was hanging on her words, waiting to find out what happened. Then the deep, masculine voice took over.

"When Pala returned, he was shocked at what he found. Men dead. Or dying. Women alone, and children abandoned completely. Ria was nowhere to be found, and all of Pala's immediate family had perished. There was fighting happening still, and he realized immediately that the population of the people had been decimated. 'Stop!' he cried out, and no one listened. 'Stop!' he cried even louder, and still, the People ignored him. Pala tore through the Village, searching for his wife. And when at last he found her, his heart broke."

The man stopped talking, and there was silence in the big room for several minutes.

"She was near death, frozen. And alone with not one, but two brand new babies, born in the snow while fighting consumed her People." Taras's voice came from right beside me again. "In her last breaths, she spoke a new prophecy for our People. A new leader would arise, and he would have to earn the title through merit instead of birth. He would have to prove himself worthy before seizing the privilege of ruling the People. He and his wife would succeed where Pala and Ria had failed. They would make the People whole. Pala renounced his role immediately, and vowed to rebuild the Village to meet both the needs of the People *and* the needs of the land. He shared Ria's prophecy, and made the requirements for future leaders very clear. He must be a man of great worth, shown in both deeds and lifestyle. He must be married to the woman prophesied by our spiritual leaders. He must be willing to sacrifice all in the name of the People. No other would ever do. And in spite of all his own success in these things, Pala never reclaimed the role. So we have gone for countless generations without naming a worthy leader. Each man living among the People both fears *and* hopes that he will be chosen. Each man hopes to be that hero, and to become king."

"Including you? Do you hope it and fear it?" The young voice cut through the silence that followed Taras's speech, and the tension broke.

Taras laughed. "Including me."

"Taras, I don't think there's *anything* that you fear," called out the feminine voice, and he laughed again.

"But you do hope," prodded the child.

"I do," Taras agreed.

"A *truly* wise man would fear it," muttered a gruff voice who hadn't spoken before.

Everyone in the big room ignored the comment, and for a second, I thought maybe I'd imagined it.

But after a moment, Taras sighed and joked, "No. A *truly* wise man knows when not to ruin a story."

The room erupted in laughter again, and Taras bumped my shoulder with his own.

"Come," he said. "There's more to do."

I followed him, reluctant to let go of the awed feeling I'd had as I listened to the story.

But by the time we came back out into the jovial atmosphere of the welcome home party in the village, I'd already lost the sensation.

***

It was too easy to lose track of time, and pretty soon my legs and head were aching. Every time we stopped, I had to lean on Taras to keep from collapsing.

During a brief lull in activity, he took my chin in his hand and tilted my head up. His intense, dark-eyed stare held mine and made my heart race.

"You're tired," he observed.

"No, I'm okay," I tried to protest, but I was swaying on my feet.

"I will take you to bed," Taras said.

I couldn't help but blush again as I looked up at him. I knew he hadn't meant it that way, but with his gaze holding mine, my thoughts immediately went there anyway. Not to mention that I felt half-drunk with tiredness. It was impossible *not* to infer innuendo.

"Where are you sleeping?" Taras asked.

"With us," Andrik said, appearing suddenly at his uncle's side.

Taras frowned. It was the first time I'd seen anything but pleasure on his face all night.

"With Gavril?" he asked.

"With Lanka," I corrected quickly.

Taras's frown deepened, but he didn't say anything.

"I'll take her home," Andrik offered.

The boy turned away for a second, distracted by something in the distance. And while his nephew was looking the other way, Taras brought his lips down to mine, feather light. It wasn't a deep kiss, or a passionate one. But it did feel nice. So I stood very still, enjoying the way he lingered there for just a moment before he stood back up straight again.

"I'll come for you tomorrow," Taras promised.

Andrik took my hand from his uncle's and pulled me away. I looked back once, just in time to see Taras disappear into a group of laughing villagers.

***

I let myself into the house and shooed Andrik away. He clearly didn't need the rest I was craving.

But I felt light-headed and giddy. My stomach was tossing nervously. I hadn't been prepared for the celebration, or Taras, or for his kiss.

I paused as I hung up my jacket, wondering if I should have reacted differently. I touched my lips with the tips of my fingers. Why *had* he kissed me? Had he been caught up in the moment? Was he just the kind of guy who kissed strange women?

Except in the Village, there *were* no strange women. Except me.

My vision swam a bit, and I knew that I'd over-extended myself.

Meeting Taras had been...interesting.

But it wasn't just that making me feel so strange. The Village had been alive tonight, and I'd felt comfortable. That worried me for a reason I couldn't pinpoint. My mind refused to focus.

"Happy?" asked a disembodied voice from inside the nearly dark house.

I jumped back, startled, and tripped over my own feet. A snorting laugh answered my clumsiness.

"Lanka?" I said. "Why are you inside?"

"I'm resting."

I didn't quite believe her, but I didn't say it.

"You met Taras," she stated.

I colored, thinking of his kiss. "Yes."

"Sit."

She lit an oil lamp and placed it in the middle of the table. I sat down across from her obediently.

"I love *both* of my sons," Lanka said slowly, as if to make sure that I had understood her words.

"Your sons?"

"Yes."

It took me a second to make the connection. "Gavril and Taras are brothers."

The relationships that existed in the village confused me. Everyone called everyone else by his or her first name. Mother and father were never used as proper nouns, though family ties were clearly important.

Lanka nodded. "Taras is a lot like his father. Handsome. Likeable. Charming. Fond of things which are new and shiny. He forces the world around him to bend to his will. Do you understand?"

I thought I'd understood. But I wanted to disagree.

Taras had seemed easygoing and considerate. Charming? Absolutely. Forceful? No way.

Lanka stared at me thoughtfully.

"Where is his father?" I asked, because I felt like she was waiting for me to say something.

"Gone."

Lanka made a sweeping hand gesture, and I knew she meant he'd died.

"I'm sorry," I said in English.

Lanka waved off my sympathy.

"Gavril is very much like *his* father, who is also gone. My first son is serious. Stubborn. Handsome, also," she told me with a smile. "I like a handsome man, so I chose two handsome ones for husbands. But Gavril is a man of tradition. He resists change, where he ought to embrace it."

Ah. They were half-brothers. It explained why they looked nothing alike.

But I disagreed with her description of Gavril, too. He was downright pushy. And mean to Nanaj. If he was traditional... Well, I wanted nothing to do with it.

Lanka nodded at me, smiling a little more, and I couldn't tell what she was thinking.

I rested my chin on the palm of my good hand. I felt guilty, and I didn't know why. Was Lanka trying to tell me something else? I didn't know her well, but she'd seemed to be nothing but straightforward with me so far.

She looked at me, expectation clear in her face.

I don't know what you're after, I wanted to say.

Then Lanka's expression changed abruptly and her eyes focused on something behind me.

"Gavril," she greeted with a nod.

I turned my head. He was standing across the room, and his face was as blank as Lanka's.

"Good night," he said stiffly.

"No. You stay. I'll go," I replied.

"Lindsay met Taras," Lanka announced.

Gavril's face clouded for a second. "I know. He told her the story."

"How did you – Oh."

The gruff voice, warning Taras that he should be fearful and hopeful...It had been Gavril's.

Why was it so important to everyone that I'd met the other man? And what would they do if they knew he kissed me?

I didn't even want to think about how they'd react. I already felt annoyed and confused, and all I wanted was to get out of the situation. Now.

I came to my feet too quickly, and dizziness hit me hard. The room swam again. Gavril said something to me, but I couldn't hear what it was.

"Drunk," I told him.

Then I frowned. *That's not right.*

I hadn't consumed anything alcoholic. I wasn't even sure if the People *had* alcohol. But I lurched forward, and that's exactly what I felt like.

Gavril shouted something angrily at Lanka. What was going on?

I lurched again.

Lanka jumped up, but she wasn't quick enough. I fell forward, landing directly at Gavril's feet.

"Hello up there," I said in a sing-song voice. "You're awfully tall, you know that?"

He had a pained looked on his face. I reached up and patted his hand in what I thought was a reassuring manner. He looked down at me, and his eyes filled with concern.

"Why are you always around when I'm in trouble?" I asked.

I didn't even know if was speaking in my own language or in theirs.

Gavril bent down, and with an ease that surprised me, he scooped me up. I couldn't hold in a giggle.

"Sorry," I apologized, but then laughed again.

Hadn't I been lucid, just a minute ago?

Gavril ignored my behaviour and pushed his way past Lanka. He carried me down the hall, right past my little room.

"Hey!" I protested. "You're kinda pushy, aren't you?"

He ignored that too, and stopped in front of the heavy-looking cloth drape that covered the door to his own room.

The beads that covered it were a dazzling array of different shapes, colours, and sizes.

I sighed appreciatively. "Pretty."

Gavril moved the drape aside with his shoulder, disregarding its splendor. He carried me into a huge room, which was divided down the middle by another curtain. One side was full of hanging shelves, covered in clay jars. The other contained a huge bed, with a well-stuffed mattress, raised by four flattened stones.

I gave the bed a suspicious glare.

"So you *did* see me naked in that tub," I accused. "What will your wife say?"

Gavril rolled his eyes. Clearly he understood at least *some* of what I was saying.

But he carried me to the side of the room without a bed and set me down gently on a cot made of tanned leather.

"I'm no lightweight, eh, Gav?" I said.

He pulled a bone knife from one of the shelves and began to cut through the long-sleeved tunic I was wearing.

"There's an easier way to get a girl undressed," I told him.

My teeth were chattering, and I realized that I was shivering uncontrollably. Gavril noticed, too, and he draped a fur blanket across my waist and then went back to cutting. When he'd exposed my bandages, he drew in a sharp breath.

I looked down. Blood had soaked through the cloth.

"Gross," I said cheerfully.

Gavril grunted and turned my injured arm up so that my wrist was pointed toward the ceiling. He cut through that fabric, too, and when he had my arm free, he began to examine my wounds with clinical professionalism. Annoyance flashed across his face.

And even I could tell that the wounds had worsened. A lot. My stitched-up gash was oozing something greenish that smelled horrible. To say that it was infected was an understatement.

"Tell me something, Gav…How are you *not* puking?" Then I leaned over and – rather unceremoniously – threw up myself.

Gavril took it in stride. He just stood and cleaned up my mess without hesitation. Then he kneeled beside me and put a hand on my forehead. He looked at my face and said something, but I didn't understand a word of it.

"I'm sorry," I said. "I seem to have broken my language button."

Gavril sighed.

"Maybe you could learn English?" I suggested hopefully.

"Lindsay," he replied, and that one word I did understand.

"Hey! That was perfect! Have you been practising?" I asked.

"Lindsay," he repeated.

His voice wrapped around my name like he was born saying it. And for some reason, that felt as good as Taras's kiss.

I wanted to say something about that, but Gavril didn't give me a chance. He was too busy pushing me down and pouring a cup of steaming hot water over my wound.

And that's when I fainted.

***

I dreamt of my mother.

"Linlin," she was saying from behind her third glass of wine. "There comes a time in every girl's life when trying new things – experimenting, if you will – stops being exciting, and starts being terrifying."

I groaned. "If this is a sex talk, you can save it. I'm twenty-eight years old."

My mother giggled, and her face went pink.

I wondered how a fifty-year-old woman could make that seem natural. She had wide-eyed, girlish innocence down to an art. Every time I blushed, I looked like I was breaking out into hives. And knowing that always made me go even redder.

A man, who was closer to my age than to hers, walked by our table and smiled at her. I groaned again as she batted her eyelashes back at him. If a free cocktail showed up in a minute or two, I wouldn't be surprised. It wouldn't be the first time, either.

"Mom," I said. "Did you call me here so that we could get drunk and you could batter me down with your wisdom, or did you actually want to talk to me about something?"

She smiled.

"I'm getting married," she announced.

"What?"

I was so sure that I'd heard wrong. She had always told me that men had three purposes. One, to lift heavy stuff. Two, to hold your purse while you peed. And three, to make babies.

Let's just say that I had a really skewed view of relationships until I was about nine. Then I had finally figured out that most mothers didn't call their kids' fathers THE DONOR.

"I'm getting married," my mom said again.

"You're... settling down?" I asked.

"If you want to call it that," she replied. "He lives in Greece."

I was forming a suspicious mental picture. It involved my mother in a gold-trimmed bikini and a dark-haired, twenty-one-year-old man we'd met in Las Vegas last year. I narrowed my eyes at her.

"Stefan?" I tried not to make it sound like an accusation.

My mom nodded agreeably.

"He's younger than I am," I protested.

"You say that like it's a bad thing," she responded.

"I'm confused," I replied desperately, trying one more time to make her see reason. "Even if we put aside your male companion policy, didn't you just tell me that trying new things was terrifying? What could be newer or more terrifying than getting married?"

She laughed. "I was talking about you, dear, not me."

I was crying when I awoke.

In real life, she hadn't said that last part. Instead she'd ignored my concern and started pouring over the details of her upcoming wedding.

I miss you, I thought.

The wound that had opened when my mother died had never even *started* to heal, and at random moments, certain things would trigger my memories of her, and I would feel the sadness freshly. If I smelled her floral perfume in the air, or heard her favourite song on the radio, I would become overwhelmed.

Her marriage to Stefan – whose last name I could rarely remember – had turned out to be just in time. The heart attack had taken her only six months later.

Had she died because she'd finally settled down? Or had her years of living a life without fetters just finally caught up to her? Or was the whole thing just a coincidence? I never decided on an answer.

At the time, Ben wasn't able to deal with my grief, so I'd always kept it closely bottled up when he was around. Maybe that had slowed the healing, too.

I inhaled deeply, and the breath I drew was ragged, and brought with it an odd mix of smells. Leather. Spices. Dirt. Sweat. My eyes flew open, and I saw that Gavril was watching me.

"Hello," I croaked.

He came to my side, emotion clouding his features momentarily. Concern which became relief which became tenderness. And then he settled on the blank stare that he seemed to prefer.

He slid an arm under my shoulders and propped me up with a pillow.

"Lindsay," he said.

I avoided his eyes. I didn't want him to know that I'd been crying.

"Lindsay," he repeated, and I looked around the room instead.

I was in his bed, I realized with embarrassment. So where had *he* been sleeping?

Gavril reached down and grabbed my chin. The gesture instantly reminded me of Taras and his gentle kiss. I flushed.

Had the brothers talked about me? I wondered.

I hoped not.

I tried to avert my eyes from his scrutiny, but Gavril made sure that I couldn't to look away, and he held up four fingers.

"Asleep," he told me, and closed his eyes dramatically.

I gasped. I'd slept for *four* days? It had felt like minutes.

Gavril stood up, went behind the curtain that divided the room, and then reappeared with a large mug of liquid. I eyed it suspiciously, and when he caught the look on my face, he took an exaggerated swig of his own.

"Okay," I relented. "Give it over."

He handed it to me, and I took a cautious sip. It was a lightly spiced, lukewarm meat broth. The same stuff Lanka had fed me right after they'd rescued me. It didn't taste like it was contaminated by anything else, so I took another small sip.

Gavril rolled his eyes, and I gave him a dirty look.

I took a large gulp defiantly.

He laughed out loud. It was that same rich laugh I'd heard from him before. It filled the room and in spite of my general dislike of the man, it made me want to smile back.

"I can't win with you, can I?" I asked in English.

He watched me drink the rest of the broth in silence, a small smile still playing on his lips. When I was done, he took the mug away and sat beside me on the bed. He grasped my injured arm gently and began to unravel the bandages. I watched his face as he did it. His jaw was set in concentration, but his eyes were still twinkling with amusement.

"It's not that funny," I muttered.

When he was done, Gavril didn't try to force me to look as Lanka had. Instead, he just gave me an expectant nod and pointed at my exposed arm.

I glanced down, and the changed state of my wrist and hand startled me.

The haphazard stitches were gone, and in their place was a tidy row of tight, even-looking ones. My gash had calmed from a swollen, oozing mess, to a reddish line. The cauterized flesh where my fingers had been removed had a scrubbed, puckered look. The splint was still there, but new skin, thin and vulnerable, was growing over my wounds.

How had that happened?

I looked up at Gavril, and I knew that he had somehow done it.

"Thank you," I whispered.

He met my gaze and nodded curtly before re-wrapping my hand.

"Better," he stated, and then left the room.

And my mind was reeling with new questions.

Chapter Six

"You have to let me up," I commanded in English.

Gavril ignored me, as he usually did.

"Up?" I repeated, appealing to him in his own language.

He sighed loudly.

He'd been keeping close tabs on me for two days, turning away anyone who tried to come through the drape, and making me eat every meal in bed. He'd let Nanaj in once to wash my hair, and he'd glowered over her the whole time while she did it. I'd half expected him to grab the soap and water and finish the job himself.

"Damn you, Gavril," I muttered. "A girl can't stay trapped in bed all day with only a man like you to entertain her."

As soon as the words were out of my mouth, I realized how they sounded. And also that I'd said them in the People's language.

But Gavril didn't look amused. He looked annoyed.

"I didn't save you from freezing to death so that you could die from over-exposing yourself to my brother."

I opened my eyes wide with surprise. It was more words than he'd spoken to me in forty-eight hours. Although I had to admit that he wasn't avoiding my company – just my conversation.

Aside from the hair wash, he'd done everything for me himself. He even slept on the cot next door, and I was beginning to really feel the lack of privacy.

Of course, I knew that it was really *me* invading *Gavril's* space, and not the other way around, but it still irritated me to be under constant surveillance.

Gavril didn't seem interested in making the extra effort to communicate with me unless it directly involved the care of my arm. And I still resented everything about him.

"I'm hungry," I lied.

He turned to me with a doubtful frown.

"Okay, I'm not hungry," I admitted and then added in English, "But I'm bored."

Gavril grunted.

"Please?" I said.

"No."

"Why are you keeping me here?"

"Where would you go?"

"Home."

Gavril snorted. "A few days of rest won't make the difference between rescue and not rescue."

At his words, a tiny bubble of hope floated to the surface. If Gavril, king of all things miserable, thought there was still a chance I could be saved...He was watching me intently, and I shoved down the momentary buoyancy.

"Not rescue?" I replied sarcastically. "Even *I* know bad grammar when I hear it."

"You have a bad temper," he told me.

"Are you being serious right now?"

"Yes."

"I feel like a prisoner."

He muttered something under his breath. It sounded like, *"Taras will not be your hero."*

"What do you have against him?"

"Who?" he said innocently.

"Your brother."

He sighed again, even more loudly. "I have to leave."

"Can I come?"

"No."

"I'll sneak out while you're gone," I warned him in English.

"I know what you're thinking, even if I don't understand your words," he said with narrowed eyes. "And I want you to *stop* thinking it."

"Fine," I muttered.

"Nanaj will come to keep you company," Gavril told me.

"To guard me, is more like it," I said under my breath.

But I was secretly relieved.

In spite of the fact that he was tending to my wounds, I still didn't like Gavril, and I was sure that he didn't like me either. He was very good at letting me know it, too.

"You know what, Gavril? You've got unpleasantness down to an art," I informed him snidely.

But he was already going through the bead-covered curtain. I leaned my head back against Gavril's bed and closed my eyes.

"He's not great with good-byes."

My eyes flew open.

"Hi, Nanaj," I sighed.

"You're doing well?"

"Well enough. But I don't know why you put up with him."

I meant the words lightly, but I saw her wince, and I felt bad. I'd seen how he treated her, and it was no joking matter.

"Love," she replied. "And a great deal of patience."

She came over to the bed and handed me a bowl of soup. And as I ate, she tidied up around me, complaining good-naturedly about the mess. When she had things done to her satisfaction, she came over to me and began brushing the tangles out of my hair with a bone-handled brush. I let her do it, just in case Gavril had ordered her to make me presentable. I didn't feel like causing another fight between them.

"It's a pretty color," she said.

I studied Nanaj's own deep brown hair. It was long, and straight, and probably never got dried out or horribly knotted like mine.

"I'd gladly trade you," I told her, and she smiled.

She took my empty soup bowl and replaced it with a pot of steaming water. She rolled up her sleeves, and I winced at the sight of a large, fresh-looking bruise on her forearm.

"Ouch," I said, pointing at it as she dipped a cloth into the water. "What happened?"

Nanaj paused with the cloth halfway to my face and smiled stiffly.

"Don't worry. Gavril is a good healer," she told me firmly, and began gently scrubbing my forehead.

I felt a chill. What was she saying? That *he* had given her the bruise? I met her eyes questioningly, and she shook her head.

"You should rest," she said.

But I had a sick feeling in my stomach.

"Why?" I asked.

"So that you can get better," Nanaj replied.

"No. I mean, why would you let someone do that to you?"

She sighed. "It's complicated. My husband has a great deal of anger to expend, and sometimes his hands get to work before his brain catches up."

"On you?"

"On the world."

"And you let him?"

"No, I don't." She sounded a little exasperated.

I gave her a disbelieving look.

"This is the worst it's been," she added.

"But you stay," I stated, ignoring the look on her face.

"Not for much longer, Lin-zee," she told me softly. "Once the baby comes... I just don't want Andrik to be alone while I'm recovering from childbirth."

"I want you to promise me," I said.

She sighed.

"*I'll* watch Andrik," I volunteered.

"And if your people come to claim you?" She smiled.

"I won't go. Or you can come with me." It was a spontaneous offer, but it was also a sincere one.

"That's a big commitment," Nanaj pointed out.

"Whatever it takes to get you away from him," I replied.

She looked like she was going to say something else, but Gavril came in at that moment.

"You may go," he told her dismissively.

I grabbed Nanaj's hand without looking at Gavril.

"Can you come back soon?" I asked.

"Yes," she replied. "I can do that."

And she left me alone with a very annoyed-looking Gavril.

"You're not taking Nanaj anywhere," he told me coldly. "Her, or anyone else. And you shouldn't make promises you can't keep."

"And you shouldn't be eavesdropping," I muttered in English. "Or hurting people who love you."

Gavril turned away, but I knew from the set of his jaw that he'd got the gist of what I'd said. And I was glad.

***

I didn't speak to him for two more days. I couldn't even make myself meet his eyes. But I watched every move he made. He mixed poultices, and cut up bandages. He changed the dressing on my wounds, and he served my meals.

He pretended to sleep, and so did I.

And every time I looked at him, all I could see was the bruise on Nanaj's arm.

On the third day, he finally felt the need to talk to me.

"I need to leave again," he announced.

I ignored him.

"It's just for a while," he added. "And I want a promise that you're not going to try to leave."

No way was I promising him that. Or anything else.

Gavril came to the bed and leaned over me. "Lindsay."

I stared past his face, examining the ceiling.

"I'll send Nanaj to keep you company," he told me, sounding more tired than mad.

I continued to look straight up, listening as he got organized. Waiting as he paused at the door.

Just go already, I thought.

Finally, I heard him exhale, then the curtain snapped, and I breathed out myself, taking a minute to enjoy the momentary solitude.

Seconds later, I felt a weight join me on the edge of the bed.

Right. Nanaj.

I opened my eyes and smiled at her. Her rounded belly was sticking out of her thick parka, and her hood was still pulled up.

"What did he drag you away from?" I asked.

She didn't answer, and I saw her shoulders shake. I sat up straighter.

"Are you crying?" I wanted to know.

Her shoulders shook harder, and I inhaled sharply.

"It's not your fault," I told her. "You know that, right?"

I tossed my blankets back, and slid over to put my arm around her waist. She tossed the hood back, and I almost yelped in surprise.

It wasn't Nanaj at all. It was Taras.

"What are you *doing*?" I hissed.

He was laughing too hard to answer. Instead, he unbuttoned his coat, pulled out a wadded up blanket, and tossed it on the floor.

"Taras?"

He put his hand over his own mouth, trying to contain himself.

"What did you do to my brother?" he asked in between laughs.

"What?"

"I think he truly believed I was Nanaj," Taras replied. "Truly. And he's not easily fooled. I fully expected to get caught."

"I didn't do anything," I protested.

"I have never seen him look so troubled."

"It wasn't me," I said.

"I don't believe it."

"I swear. I haven't even spoken to him in two days."

Taras grinned, and after I minute, I smiled back.

"I'm sure Gavril deserves it," Taras stated.

"You have no idea," I replied in English.

But my heart dropped a little as I said it. Maybe he did have an idea. Maybe it was normal in the village for a man to hit his wife the way Gavril hit Nanaj.

Taras touched my cheek. "Don't be sad."

"I'm not," I lied.

He leaned forward and kissed my mouth gently, his hand still on my face. His other arm slid around my waist, and I was suddenly very aware that I was wearing nothing but a long tunic. Part of me wanted to pull away, and part of me wanted to lean in and demand more. Oddly, I felt tears form in my eyes, and then dribble embarrassingly down my cheeks. Taras pulled back, and wiped them away with his thumb.

Someone cleared their throat from the other side of the beaded curtain, and I jerked away from Taras.

"Hello, Nanaj," he greeted without turning away from me. "It's nice to see the *real* you."

A giggle died in my throat as she came in. A large red welt marked one of her cheekbones. Taras caught sight of it at the same second I did, and he stood up angrily.

"No, Taras," Nanaj said quietly.

"This is unacceptable," Taras replied. "He told me that he would stop. Swore on his father's name, in fact."

So he does *know*, I thought. *And he doesn't like it.*

That was a relief, at least.

"I'm okay," Nanaj insisted.

Taras pulled his parka on and glared, suddenly looking an awful lot like his brother.

"Gavril will answer for this," he stated coldly. "It's gone on for too long, and I can no longer allow it."

He touched my hand briefly, then stalked out of the room.

Nanaj sat on the edge of the bed, and I held her as she began to cry.

***

Minutes later, Gavril came storming back into the room.

"Dress. And come," Gavril barked at me.

He rounded on Nanaj, who was resting on the cot. She looked up at him nervously, and covered the red mark on her face with her hand.

"How dare you involve Taras in this once again? I've told you to leave him and Lanka out of it," he yelled.

"It wasn't her," I said.

He turned back to me. "Was it you?"

"No."

His face was so hard that it could've been carved of stone.

"Nanaj needs to take care of her own problems," he told me.

"*Her* problems?" I replied sarcastically.

"Dress, Lindsay. Now." His tone left no room for argument. "You wanted to go out. We're going out."

I dressed as quickly as I could and followed him out, putting my parka on silently. I was half-afraid to speak, worried about what his reaction might be. I was already worried enough that he was taking out his anger at me on Nanaj.

When we were outside at last, I took a deep breath and looked around. It had been more than a week since I'd left Gavril's house, and the village had changed.

Only half of the large oil lamps that lined the pathway were lit, but I could still see. It was almost, but not quite, bright enough to pass for twilight. I felt as much relief at that as I did at my quasi-release.

"Come on," Gavril said, and I had to scramble to keep up with him.

He led me to another entryway, and I followed him inside. He didn't speak – he just pulled out two lamps, then hung them from the ceiling.

The space, which wasn't much bigger than Gavril's bedroom, was full of jars, cups, blankets, and tools that I didn't recognize. It brought to mind evil scientists and Frankenstein's monster. I shivered.

He pointed, and I was surprised that there were two wooden chairs in the room. Wood was so precious a commodity that it seemed strange to find it there.

"Sit," he suggested without explanation.

"So much for freedom," I muttered.

But it was still marginally better than being bedridden.

Gavril turned to me, irritation and frustration clear on his face. Was he going to try and justify his abusive relationship? Was he going to tell me that it was complicated, like Nanaj had?

"I'm sorry that you had to see what a man's anger can lead to," he said.

I didn't reply, and he tried again.

"This marriage doesn't suit Nanaj. It never has."

"That's a copout if I ever heard one," I told him in English.

He grunted.

"You blame *her*?" I asked, switching back to his language.

"Not completely."

Gavril gave my incredulous stare a big sigh.

"If she wishes to leave, she should just do it," he said.

"She thinks it's love," I replied angrily. "Why don't you tell her it's not?"

"I don't pretend to understand anything to do with love." Gavril sounded bitter.

"No kidding."

He looked wounded, and I was glad.

"What?" I demanded defiantly.

"I can no longer care for you and no one else," Gavril told me.

His words confused me. But only for a second. Because at that moment, his first patient arrived.

For three more days, I followed Gavril back and forth from the dimly lit underground structure, and I quickly realized that he wasn't just my healer. He was the healer for the entire village.

He still wasn't much of a talker, even when dealing with his patients, and I felt a little better about how seldom he spoke to me. And all of the People who came in made up for Gavril's relative silence. They all loved to talk and they were excited to have a sympathetic ear. They seemed delighted with how easily I'd learned to communicate with them.

I figured out, also, why Gavril had been so adept at caring for my wounds. Almost every patient was either a burn victim – mostly minor – or had some type of cut. Gavril stitched them all up with care, applied effective poultices to their blisters, then turned them out with repeated cautions to be more careful. Almost no one was sick. The only exception seemed to be some of the hunters, who had a chronic coughs from exposure to the extreme weather.

And it was hard to reconcile Gavril the healer with Gavril the man who hit his wife. He wasn't exactly pleasant, but he was rarely short-tempered, either.

The fourth day of acting as Gavril's shadow was a particularly busy one, and he had an exasperated crease etched into his brow.

Gavril finished patching up a barely visible scratch on a little boy's arm, sent him away with a stern glare at his mother, then turned to me with an irritated glare.

"What?" I said, glaring back.

"I think they're hurting themselves on purpose," he muttered.

I frowned, puzzled. Even though it was getting easier and easier for me to communicate with the People, I was sure that I'd misunderstood him.

"What?" I repeated.

"So that they can see *you*," he explained. "Never before has the same girl burned herself on soup three times in one day. But it's happened to *four* girls since you have been here."

I grinned, and Gavril's glare deepened.

"Am I supposed to apologize?" I wanted to know.

"It couldn't hurt," he agreed.

"You're forcing me to stay here with you," I reminded him. "And forcing me to sleep in your bed. And you won't even let me talk to anyone who isn't a patient."

"Who would you talk to?" he wanted to know.

My face reddened as my mind went immediately to Taras.

"Nanaj," I answered quickly.

Gavril looked like he was about to call my bluff, but a young woman carrying a little boy with a bloody nose came in at just that moment.

I stepped away, and let him tend to the child. He did it quickly, then ushered them out before turning back to me.

"You need to rest. You don't seem to do it on your own. I won't have Taras dragging you around in the cold," Gavril said.

"Stop being so stubborn. You could let me go back to picking rocks with Andrik," I suggested.

"You would have died," he reminded me bluntly. "If it hadn't been for my *stubbornness*."

I coloured. "Thank you for saving me. Twice."

He shrugged. "I don't believe I had a choice."

What does that mean? I wondered.

But the frown on his face stopped me from asking.

"What do you want me to do?" I said instead.

"You could try being a little less distracting," he suggested.

"What do you mean I could be..." I trailed off as the tent flap opened once more.

Nanaj, looking even more pregnant than usual, stood there hesitantly, looking from me to Gavril.

"Hello, Nanaj," Gavril greeted abruptly.

It was the first time I'd seen her since Taras's angry reaction to her bruises, and since Gavril's responding outburst. She and Andrik had been sleeping elsewhere. And I didn't blame them.

Gavril placed his hands on his hips, and Nanaj stared at him with wide eyes. He did look very intimidating at that moment, glowering and annoyed.

"Jerk," I said in English.

Nanaj turned to me.

"Come in," I suggested warmly to the other woman.

She stepped further into Gavril's workspace, smiling at me.

Gavril met my eyes and gave me a look that said, *I told you so.*

"I suppose you've hurt yourself. Again," he said sarcastically.

She touched the little welt on her face self-consciously. It looked better, but it wasn't healed yet.

"She didn't do that to herself," I muttered.

"I'll get you some more salve," he told Nanaj, ignoring me.

"I'm not very hurt," she replied. "And I don't need your salve. I came to invite Lin-zee to have dinner with me."

"Oh!" I said, pleased. "I'd like that. A lot."

Gavril's mouth tightened.

"I'm fine," I informed him.

He looked like he wanted to argue, but he sighed and nodded instead.

"I'll walk her there when we're done," he said in a resigned and dismissive voice to Nanaj.

The other woman exited Gavril's office and he turned to me.

"Eat," he commanded, "And then come right back."

"You could be nicer," I retorted.

"To Nanaj? Or to you?"

"Both!" I snapped.

I felt tears form suddenly in my eyes. I blinked them back self-consciously and drew in a breath.

Gavril stepped toward me, concern playing across his features.

"Are you in pain?" he asked.

"I don't know why you care."

"It's my job to care."

"I miss my life," I answered in English.

He frowned, looking annoyed. I decided that I liked it better when he *hadn't* been talking to me. At least I hadn't had to put up with his bad attitude then.

He turned away and began fiddling with the jars on his shelves.

"I think that you're much better," he said. "I'm going to have Lanka find a job for you. Away from here."

"Good," I replied loudly, still speaking English.

Gavril spun around, and his eyes were flashing. I snorted. Now what was he mad about? That I *wanted* to go? What was his problem?

"Seriously?" I said, still refusing to use his language.

I had asked him questions, and he hadn't answered them. I hadn't brought up Taras, since it so obviously bothered him, and I hadn't even tried to talk to him about his relationship with Nanaj. Not since the first day, anyway. I'd also tried to help him with his patients, and he'd brushed off my assistance. I was stuck here with his violent temper, and his general resentment of me. I was stuck with *him*. But he was just going about his day-to-day business.

He had no right to be mad.

I grabbed my parka and shrugged into it. I wasn't going to let him hold me prisoner for a second longer. Gavril spun around, dropping a small jar. It shattered, but he ignored it and strode toward me.

I looked up at him. He was tall, and wide, and momentarily ferocious-looking. He was also blocking the exit. He clenched his hands into fists and held them at his sides.

I stared down at his balled-up fists with fear. I'd seen how those hands worked, stitched, cleaned, and healed. They were nimble and strong. Gavril had used them to fix me. And yet, I had seen his wife's bruised arm. And her face.

I dragged my gaze up to meet his eyes.

His expression was unreadable, as it so often was. The flashes of emotion that I'd seen over the last few minutes were buried somewhere underneath his mask once again.

"What are you hiding?" I whispered.

Then Gavril's face changed. It became overwhelmed with feeling instead of devoid of it. Sorrow. Anger. Pain.

And something else.

I stepped forward, and for a second, I imagined his arms coming up around me, crushing me against his chest. I imagined him pulling me close, using one hand to hold me against his hip and the other to cup my cheek. I could almost feel his mouth smashing into mine.

I didn't want to be picturing it.

I shouldn't want it.

He was cruel and horrible and Nanaj was my friend.

Except...I *did* want it. And almost...I thought I might want *him.*

Oh, god. What is wrong *with me?*

My body tensed in nervous anticipation.

But Gavril stepped back with a ragged breath.

"What makes you so good at this?" he demanded.

"What?" I couldn't keep the catch out of my voice.

Gavril shook his head. "How do you come to a place, knowing nothing, and so quickly learn to be a part of it?"

I didn't have the words to answer, and he just stared at me, eyes burning.

He gave up and grabbed his jacket. He buttoned it quickly, and exited the tent so fast that I had to really scramble to catch up.

I followed him as best I could, grateful that we were still in a perpetual state of dusk so that my flush was invisible to the people who were watching us with interest.

Gavril stopped abruptly in front of one of the houses.

"Nanaj will want you to eat here," he told me stiffly.

"Thanks."

I was infuriated by Gavril's behaviour, and even more stunned by my reaction to him. For a split second, I had been *so* sure that he was going to kiss me. And I had really wanted it. In spite of the fact that I knew his temper, and in spite of the fact that I knew his wife, and in spite of the fact that I knew what happened when those two things got mixed together.

But he seemed unaware of my swirling emotions. He just nodded and stalked off in the other direction.

"What's wrong with me?" I said out loud, and then braced myself to face Nanaj.

Chapter Seven

"This is delicious," I told Nanaj for about the tenth time.

It was part truth, and part guilt.

I'd been chattering non-stop since coming inside. The home was so much less Spartan than the one where I'd been staying. There were handmade toys everywhere, and a partially sewn blanket, waiting to be finished, was draped across the floor.

"This is a nice house," I said, wondering who it belonged to. "It suits you much better than that plain old room at the other place."

"Gavril's tastes in decor are somewhat lacking," she said with a smile.

My face heated up when she said his name. I unwillingly pictured that brief second of real emotion, remembering how it changed his face. Should I confess to Nanaj what I'd felt, even if it was just for a moment? I'd been fighting with myself about it since I walked in the door.

"You're acting a little strange," Nanaj told me, interrupting my distracted thinking.

The colour in my cheeks deepened. "Sorry."

"It's okay."

"The food really *is* good."

She grinned at me.

"I'm an excellent cook," Nanaj told me a bit ruefully. "Too many years doing it. Cooking is my punishment, though Lanka refuses to admit it."

I looked at her face, trying to decide if I should smile, or frown. Her reply made me want to ask a lot of questions.

"Ask whatever you like," Nanaj suggested, easily reading my expression.

It was hard for me to pick the best line of inquiry. I had some cultural questions, and some personal ones.

I'd already figured out a few things, mostly from listening to Gavril's patients over the last few days.

The People divided the year up to two parts – the Melt and the Freeze. The men came and went, hunting in the surrounding area as weather permitted. The women stayed behind, functioning as a co-operative unit. There was a little less than two hundred People living in the village, and as I'd noted before, all of them had a defined role. Some of the jobs were based on age, and some of them on skill. I hadn't been able to determine who was in charge. Or if *anyone* was. There was a lot more to learn, but now that I'd been given free rein to inquire, I was drawing a blank.

And then there was the issue of Gavril, and his overeager fists.

"Punishment for what?" I finally asked.

"Marrying without Lanka's approval," she replied.

"I don't blame her for her disapproval," I said, then frowned. "What is *Lanka's* job, exactly?"

Nanaj laughed. "To boss the People around. She works with the master storytellers. Do you remember those two cranky older ladies who squeezed your sore hand?"

"How could I forget?"

"Duscna and Jereni help Lanka interpret our stories and apply them to our daily life. Each new generation has new stories. For Lanka's part of interpretation, that means work assignments and weddings."

"Does Lanka arrange everyone's marriages?" I replied.

"She doesn't arrange," Nanaj told me. "She approves. Or does not approve."

"I see."

"She didn't approve of Elak, but I persisted." Nanaj made a face. "And it's sad that Lanka is so often right."

"Who's Elak?" I asked, confused.

"My husband."

I stared at her. "Elak?"

"Yes. The one who gave me this." She pointed at the mark on her face.

"Wait. Nanaj…Gavril isn't your husband?"

"What?"

Now *she* looked utterly confused.

"He's not your husband?"

Nanaj laughed loudly. "No! Gavril is my brother."

"But what you said about love and patience…"

"Still applies," she said. "And believe it or not, my brother needs it even more than my husband does."

"So he doesn't hit you?"

"Gavril?" She sounded almost horrified. "No. He's a healer. A good one. Didn't I tell you that?"

"I thought you were just defending him."

My new friend shifted slightly, and pushed up her sleeves to her elbows. I gasped. Her arms were covered in more fresh bruises. She smiled sadly.

"I would *never* defend this," she told me. "And Gavril – he would hurt himself before he'd hurt someone else. But it hasn't always been this way with Elak, either. He threw words long before he threw fists."

She seemed so calm about it. Not resigned, not regretful. Just matter-of-fact. She really *wasn't* trying to defend him.

"You're still wondering how a woman like me stays with a man like him," she stated.

I nodded.

"At first I hoped he would change. Then I was too stubborn to go," she replied. "Now I've made my bed. And I will lie in it for at least a short time longer."

"I don't really understand."

"Once the baby is born, I'll petition to be released from my marriage."

"Taras said that he was going to have Gavril take care of it," I told her, recalling his words with a new understanding of what they meant.

"My brothers disagree on many things," she said. "The least of which is how to deal with my husband. Gavril feels that I should leave on my own. Taras feels that my hand should be forced."

"What do you think?" I asked.

"Both of my brothers are right. And our mother is seldom wrong," she said softly. "And that's why her job is what it is. I should have listened to her wishes from the start. She provides personal guidance for the women of the village, and she does it well."

"Who guides the men, then?" I asked.

I was still mulling over the fact that Gavril and Nanaj were brother and sister, not husband and wife.

"At the moment... No one," Nanaj replied seriously. "We have been without a leader for some time."

I remembered the story Taras had told on the night he'd arrived in the village.

"I know that you've been asking for a way off the People's land," she said, and I thought she might be trying to change the subject for my benefit.

"It's not that I don't appreciate the hospitality. But I just wondered why, when you live on an island like this one, there are no boats."

Nanaj looked puzzled, and I tried to explain to her what that meant, as I had done with Andrik.

She giggled a little.

"No floating houses," she informed me.

I smiled at her, but inside, I was feeling panicked. Not one of the People seemed aware of an outside world, and I was beginning to form a scary conclusion.

No evidence of modernity touched the People's culture. They had no tools made of metal. No inkling of the workings of electricity. But they were advanced at the things they needed for survival. Hunting. Building. Surviving the cold.

I was starting to suspect that the People were really, truly isolated from the rest of the world. Like the frozen version of a deserted island.

Oh no.

My brain had kicked into overdrive, but I tried to keep it from my face.

I attempted to think of another question to ask Nanaj. Hadn't I had so many? But all I could do was make a list.

No boats. No planes. No way home.

Nanaj opened her mouth, and then closed it.

I wondered if I was going to faint again.

"Are you all right?" Nanaj wanted to know.

"I don't know," I replied.

"Would you like to lie down?" she asked softly.

"Is this your house?"

She nodded. "You can even sleep here tonight, if you want."

"What about Elak?"

"Taras sent him away again this morning," she told me.

"Nanaj, how long have I been in the village?"

She was silent for moment, and then she replied, "Thirty-two days."

"How can you be so sure?"

"You can count them yourself, if you want."

"No...I believe you. I just..."

"Is that long enough to give up?" Nanaj wanted to know.

I laughed without much humor. "Shouldn't *I* be asking that question?"

"Maybe. If you didn't want to have to be honest about the answer."

"Should I give up hope?"

"I don't think you should give up *hope*," Nanaj told me. "Not ever. But at some point, you need to move on to possibilities, right?"

I couldn't argue against that.

"Would you like some strong tea?"

I shook my head. "Is that offer to lie down still open?"

"Would you like to?"

"Yes, please."

I felt a bit like I was avoiding the issue, but my head didn't want to deal with hope, with possibilities, or with giving up.

***

I woke up with knots in my back and a headache coursing through my temple. For a moment, I wondered if I was getting the flu. Then I remembered.

I'm not sick. I'm just lost.

I'd been tossing and turning, bombarded with dreams of myself standing on the edge of a beach, wearing my favourite two-piece. Only instead of sand and surf, there had been snow, and ice chips floating in the water.

"Lin-zee."

I groaned and rolled over. Even though the bedroll on Nanaj's floor wasn't anywhere near as comfortable as the pile of blankets at Gavril's house, I wasn't ready to get out of bed.

And now I was hearing voices.

"Lin-zee."

A hand stroked my hair, which I hoped was starting to look less poodle-like, and I sat bolt upright.

A dark form was leaning over my bed. I blinked, trying to push down my panic. I squinted.

"Taras?" I whispered.

He tossed his hood back and grinned his hawk-like grin. I hadn't seen him since the day he'd sneaked into my room at Gavril's house. I'd even almost forgotten how good-looking he was. But there was no way around it right that second.

I blushed in the dark.

"I'd like to spend some time with you," he said.

"What? Now?"

He nodded.

"What time *is* it?" I asked in English.

He tilted his head to the side curiously.

"Right," I said.

The People related time to either food, or to work that had to be done each day. Maybe because of the perpetual darkness. I only knew when it was morning, noon, or night because of which meal I was eating.

"Is it... " I tried to remember the word for breakfast, but my sleepy brain didn't feel like co-operating.

"It's late," he said, answering my unasked question.

"What are we going to do?"

Taras smiled slightly. "Something. Anything. But I don't believe that my brother would approve of us doing whatever it is we're going to do. Or rather, approve of me taking you out at all. So I'm glad you're here rather than there."

"He's my doctor. Not my keeper," I muttered under my breath.

Taras laughed.

"He doesn't think it's as funny as you do," I told him.

Taras frowned at my expression, and touched my cheek gently.

I wanted to ask him how he got in, but I knew there wasn't really a need. There were no locks in the village, and from what I'd seen, no one would've stopped Taras from doing what he wanted anyway.

Mr. Popularity, I thought.

The look on his face made me pretty sure that he was expecting to get his way now, too.

"Okay, fine," I agreed with a sigh.

He handed me my coat, then my mittens. As he did so, he touched the bandages on my hand gently. For a second, I thought he was going to ask to see underneath, but he just slid my glove over top.

It was the first time I'd been outside at night since I'd arrived. And for some reason, I expected it to be vastly different than the day, but except for the lack of people, it was the same. Still twilight, still lit by lamps.

Taras nodded at some sleepy-looking men who appeared to be acting as sentries. I wondered if they were there all the time. What were they guarding against? Loose reindeer?

I smiled at the thought, remembering the gentle creature who'd greeted me just after I crashed. He seemed about as dangerous as a tree.

"You have a nice smile. You should use it more often," Taras said, and I looked down at the ground.

He took my hand, and we walked in a loop around the outside of the in-ground houses. The cold didn't seem to bother Taras at all, even though it was making me shiver under my parka.

"Do you wish to go home?" Taras asked suddenly.

"I'm okay right now," I said.

"I mean *home* home."

"Oh. Yes, I do," I replied.

"Is it so much better there?"

I wanted to laugh at the look on his face. It was disbelieving and even a little petulant. Like a child worried that his friend had a better toy.

"It's just... different," I said.

"How?"

I hesitated.

Where could I start? Planes, or cars, or computers? *Would he even believe in their existence?* I wondered.

"It's…warmer," I finally stated.

He laughed. "And?"

"And lots of stuff."

Taras stopped walking and turned his penetrating stare toward me. There was something unnerving about his gaze. Its intensity *commanded* compliance. I swallowed, knowing why so many of the People were affected by his presence, and understanding what Lanka had meant when she said he bent the world around his will.

"Like what?" he persisted.

"Too many things to explain," I forced myself to say.

"Do you have a husband?"

My face warmed. "No."

"Children?"

"No."

"Do you *like* children?"

"Yes, of course."

He looked momentarily placated, and I blushed even more. We started walking again.

"Your nephew is great," I told him, feeling silly.

"He makes me proud," he agreed. "Nanaj is an excellent mother."

"Yes."

Taras stopped again, and I braced myself for another onslaught of unnerving questions, but instead he reached out and touched my face. His caress was gentle, but not hesitant. I wondered if he was going to kiss me again, as he had on the last two times we'd met.

"Lin-zee," Taras said softly, and he leaned in.

I pulled away slightly.

"Do you dislike kissing?" he asked.

"No."

"Do you dislike me?"

"No."

"Then why do you hesitate?"

Because I don't belong here, I thought.

But I sighed and said, "I don't know."

He leaned in again, and his lips met mine, ever so lightly, and then his head jerked away and he cried out. I fell back in surprise, landing on the snow with a thump.

"Taras!" hissed a familiarly angry voice.

Gavril.

I looked up. The two men were already locked in each other's grips. Gavril pressed his forehead to Taras's, and said something in a tone that was too low for me to hear. Taras tried to pull away, but his brother held him firmly. Gavril was shorter by an inch or two, but if I had to guess, I would've said that he was fifty pounds heavier. His mouth was set in a grim line, and he looked as though he could keep Taras in place for as long as he felt like it.

I cowered against the ground, unable to make out most of what they were saying. I heard my name a few times, and then the two men who had appeared to be standing guard joined us. They eyed the brothers nervously.

At last, Gavril shoved Taras away and turned to me. Taras hesitated, his gaze shifting between us.

"You gave up the right to make my decisions for me a long time ago," Taras said mildly.

Gavril fixed him with a menacing stare, and with a sigh, his brother walked away, shaking his head.

"Return to bed," Gavril growled at me.

For a split second, I considered resisting, but the look in Gavril's eye brooked no argument. He grabbed my arm and yanked me to my feet.

Gavril led me back to Nanaj's house without a word, and left me standing there in the cold.

Chapter Eight

"Good morning."

My eyes flew open, and I gazed up at Andrik's smiling face.

"Good morning yourself," I replied, being careful to keep the anxiety out of my voice.

The rest of the night hadn't been kind to me. I kept playing the scene from the previous night over and over again in my head.

Had anyone besides the guards seen what had happened? Did they care?

And what exactly *had* happened, anyway?

Andrik sat down with a grin, and I gave my head a little shake.

"How have you been?" I asked.

"When did you learn to talk properly?" he demanded.

"You sound disappointed," I observed.

Andrik shrugged. "I like your funny words."

"Funny words?" I repeated in English, and he grinned.

"Are you still sick?" he wanted to know.

"Sick?"

He pointed to my hand and made a face.

"Not so much," I replied.

"Good," Andrik said in English.

I laughed. "How did you know where to find me?"

"I went to Gavril's to get you, but you weren't there. He said you were probably here," Andrik told me.

"Now that I'm feeling better... Are we collecting rocks again today?"

He shook his head sadly. "Lanka said if you were better, you would have to start doing a grown-up job."

"Lanka's not at Gavril's?"

"She was at Taras's house," Andrik explained.

Oh.

"Did she seem... unhappy?" I asked carefully.

"No. Why?"

"No reason."

"*I'm* unhappy, though," Andrik said, accepting my casual deflection. "Because you're not going to be able to spend as much time with me if you're doing a grown-up job."

I sat up and reached over to ruffle his hair.

"We can do something else together," I offered.

"Like what?" He sounded forlorn.

"How about we start with breakfast?" I suggested.

Andrik grinned again, sat down on my bed, and pulled two thick-looking buns out of his pocket. He handed me one, and I took a big bite, ignoring the bits of fuzz that clung to the surface.

"Hit the spot perfectly," I told him in English. "Thank you."

"I'm supposed to take you to Lanka," Andrik said as soon as we finished eating.

"Am I allowed to put clothes on first?" I teased.

"Okay," he agreed, and let himself out of my room so that I could get ready.

I got dressed quickly. I was getting better at using my damaged hand, now that it was really starting to heal.

Thanks to Gavril, I added mentally before I could stop myself.

"Done!" I called to Andrik.

"Hurry," he replied, and I decided to comply.

I knew that Lanka had probably been up for hours, and after Nanaj's wry comments about punishment, I didn't want to put her in a bad mood right before she assigned me a job.

I followed Andrik out into the chilly air. It seemed a little lighter than it had the day before, and I wondered how long it would be before we saw some actual sun. We walked past Gavril's door, and I frowned to cover my blush.

The previous evening seemed like a bad dream.

I wanted to ask Andrik where we were going, but I didn't trust myself to be able to keep the embarrassed tremor out of my voice, and I didn't need to be asked any awkward questions. He was a very intuitive kid.

My little friend guided me to an unfamiliar home, and I looked down at the doorway in surprise. The outside tent flap was dyed a dark red, and a horseshoe-shaped decoration, woven intricately with some kind of pliable wood, hung above the door.

"Whose house if this?" I asked.

"My other uncle's," Andrik told me.

Oh. Taras's house.

I wondered if I should even be there.

"Come in, please," Andrik said politely.

He led me through the flaps, and as I entered the house, I was immediately struck by how different it was from Gavril's place. The walls were covered with the same kind of material, but instead of being neutral in colour, they were dyed to varying shades of brown – from the lightest tan, to a colour that reminded me of a forest floor. Trinkets and wreaths hung from pegs on every wall, and a spear dangled menacingly above the in-ground fireplace.

"Do you like it?" Andrik asked shyly.

"It's very pretty," I agreed.

"I helped decorate," Andrik announced proudly.

Lanka snorted from her spot on a cushy-looking floor pillow.

"My youngest son likes pretty things. And so does my grandson," she said dryly. "You may go, Andrik."

He scrambled to get back out of the house, leaving me to eye Lanka warily. I wasn't sure how I felt about her assigning a job for me.

"He wants me to find a place for you," she informed me.

"Who does?" I asked.

"Gavril. He thought you'd wandered off into the snow last night. He was looking for you."

"He did? He was?"

Well, at least that explained his behaviour. It didn't excuse it, but at least it was something other than jealousy.

I felt myself flush at the idea. Had I really thought that was the source of his action?

Maybe, I admitted silently.

Lanka was nodding again. "And now he says that if you are well enough to go for late walks with Taras, you are well enough to have a job."

"As if it's up to him," I said irritably.

The older woman smiled in agreement.

"I *will* put you somewhere," she told me. "But because I want to. Not because Gavril says it must be so."

"Any chance I can get you to put me home?" I asked in English.

Lanka narrowed her eyes. "You must speak the language of the People."

"But I'm not one of the People," I replied softly.

Lanka's expression softened. "I will help you get there."

"Every time I talk about leaving, you change the subject," I said.

"Do I?"

I nodded. "Everyone does. That, or they tell why I should stay. Except Nanaj."

"My daughter can be foolish."

"At least she's honest."

"Your presence is... Unnerving for the People. Frightening, even," Lanka explained with sigh.

"Me? Frightening?" I almost laughed.

"You dropped out of the air." Lanka pointed up for emphasis. "How do you suppose we go about getting you back up there?"

I felt despair overwhelm me, and I took a shaky breath. I might never go home. And I might never fit in here.

"There has to be way off the island," I said, sounding desperate.

"None that I know of," Lanka replied.

I sagged.

"We have an expression," Lanka said gently. "We say that you must take each day as it is, and the next day as it will be."

"One day at a time?" I asked.

Lanka nodded.

"We have the same expression where I come from," I told her.

She smiled at me. "Come. You are about to learn what it truly means to be one of the People."

***

Over the next few days, Lanka gave me a crash course in the various jobs available in the village. She started off small, having me fetch snow for melting. This was done by a group of giggling, pre-school-aged kids, and was overseen by two friendly adolescent boys. She let me work with Andrik for part of a day – more for his sake than for my learning experience, I thought. She sent me on a hike with a group of teenagers. We walked to an area that they seemed to know well. It was a shaded dip in the tundra, where a vine-like shrub grew along the ground under the cover of the snow. They dug, and picked up dried or already-dead pieces of the woody substance and deposited them into satchels for returning to the village. Lanka had someone guide me through the large, in-ground structure where the People treated a grassy plant and then processed it into the linen that made the bulk of their clothes. She had the same person show me the area where they would tan the reindeer hides in the summer. It was all interesting, and all overwhelming.

I went home tired after each excursion. We continued to stay at Gavril's, and even though I hadn't seen him at all, I felt like I was taking up an unwelcome place in his home. I half-wondered if he was avoiding me.

But then again, I hadn't spied Taras either. And I had only seen Nanaj once.

Lanka kept me far too busy for a social life.

We ate dinner early each evening, and she reported to me on my progress.

One afternoon, she told me not to sit down.

"You can melt snow," she said with a grin. "You can make a clay cup. You can build a fire."

"Sort of," I agreed, wondering what was coming next.

Melting snow was the only one of those three things I felt really confident about doing.

"Can you cook a meal?" Lanka asked

I thought suddenly of my signature lasagne, all draped in gooey cheese, and of Greek salad, bathed in mouth-watering oil.

"I can. At home," I said.

Lanka frowned momentarily. "You *are* home."

I opened my mouth and then closed it again.

Home has running water and flush toilets and the Internet, I wanted to tell her.

But I kept my thoughts to myself.

"Today, you cook," Lanka said.

Uh-oh. I dreaded the idea of going into strangers' homes to prepare their meals.

Lanka laughed at the expression on my face.

"Only here, and only for me," she explained, and I relaxed. "I'm even going to help you. I already collected the ingredients."

"Where do you keep them, normally?" I wanted to know.

Lanka gestured toward an alcove behind the cook fire. "Some things are stored. Some are delivered."

I grinned, imagining the cost of having food hand-delivered every day at home.

Lanka handed me a basket full of rooty vegetables and a partially frozen fish.

"Stew?" I asked, and Lanka nodded.

She helped me chop the vegetables with a bone knife, and showed me how to clean and gut the fish. Then she grabbed a large clay pot, and she explained that we had to soak it in water before tossing everything into it.

"The water stops the pot from drying out and breaking," she told me. "Plus, it holds the flavour in."

She handed me a fitted lid, and we placed the pot right onto the hot coals.

"Now what?" I wanted to know.

"Now we make the bread," Lanka replied.

She handed me a bowl made of stiffened hide. It was full of coarse flour.

"This is easy," she said.

"Easier than making a fire?" I asked.

"Much," she agreed with a smirk.

She gave me a clay jar, and when I opened it, I saw that it was brimming with murky-looking sea salt.

"Stir with your hand," Lanka instructed.

I used my undamaged hand to mix the ingredients together, and pretty soon I had a nicely textured dough, made simply from the flour, salt, and warm water.

"Watch now," Lanka said.

She produced a long, skinny stick that reminded me of a marshmallow roaster. She wound a thick rope of the dough around the end, then tossed some water onto the coals beside the stew pot. She held the stick in the outflow of steam, and I watched in amazement as the dough bubbled, expanded, and turned golden. She pulled the stick out and pried the bread off.

"Eat it," she suggested.

It was crispy and good, and my mouth watered with the anticipation of dipping it in my stew.

"The young cooks like to make the bread on a clay tray," Lanka told me a little disdainfully. "But this way is better."

I agreed.

We made six more pieces of the steamed bread, and set it aside to be eaten with the stew.

When we were finally done, I sat down at the table with a big sigh. I was tired. My muscles ached from all the physical labour I'd been doing. I was entirely unused to it.

"Feeling sorry for yourself?" Lanka asked.

"A little," I admitted.

"Tomorrow, I will let you do some real grown-up work," she told me.

"Thank you?" I said it like a question, and Lanka laughed.

"Taras will be back in the morning. And Gavril, too," she informed me, and there was a question there, too.

"I didn't realize they were gone."

It explained why I hadn't seen them at all.

"They went off. Gathering things... " Lanka trailed off, and I knew I was supposed to ask for more information.

"What things?" I prodded obligingly.

"Berries. Seeds. Medicines. Things that do not grow near here, but can be plentiful in the right areas."

"Oh."

Lanka made an exasperated noise.

"Don't you wonder why we don't move ourselves closer to these things?" she asked.

"I wonder a lot of things," I replied.

Lanka rolled her eyes.

"The People are not alone," she told me menacingly, and I would have laughed if she hadn't looked so serious.

You have no idea, I thought.

I waited for further explanation, but Lanka stood abruptly. I opened my mouth, and the older woman shook her head.

"I can see that you're not ready."

"Not ready for what?"

But it was easy to read her expression.

End of discussion.

At least for now.

"I believe the stew is ready," she said, and handed me the bowls to dish it up.

Chapter Nine

I slept deeply and dreamlessly, and for the first time since my crash landing, I got out of bed without being woken up. The house was quiet, and I knew that I was the only one up.

I walked out into the eating area, set out a stack of clay plates, located the berry jam, and dug out the ingredients to make some more bread.

I was struck by sudden inspiration, and I mixed the jam right into the dough before I started to cook it. I hummed as I worked, pleased with myself.

"Well," said a deep voice from behind me. "This is *not* what I expected to see."

I jumped, and whirled around to see Taras standing at the door with an amused smile on his face.

"Um. Hi," I said awkwardly.

"When Lanka invited me for a meal, I didn't think that she meant you would be making it."

"Sorry," I replied, embarrassed. "But I learned how to make bread."

"That's good news."

"We'll *see* if it's good news," Lanka stated as she appeared in the eating area.

Taras didn't hide his amusement. "You can go ahead and *see*. I'm going to *taste*."

Andrik appeared beside his uncle, and Nanaj was close behind him. She ushered her son to the table, squeezing my arm as she went by. They both sat down at the table, making a big fuss over my creation.

"Delicious," Andrik told me in English, and I grinned.

I sat back to enjoy their chatter, and I was so engrossed in a story that Andrik was telling – something about a baby fox he'd found out near his trove of rocks – that I almost missed it when Taras whispered in my ear.

"Do you want to go for a walk?" he asked.

"What?"

"A walk?" he repeated more loudly, and the rest of the table went quiet.

I didn't know where Gavril was, but I was suddenly glad that he wasn't there.

I looked down at my hands.

"I thought you might tend vegetables today with Nanaj," Lanka said.

"You did?"

"That's what Lanka told me yesterday," Nanaj confirmed.

I didn't know what to say. I felt almost like they were discouraging me from accepting Taras's offer. Had Gavril got to them? I sighed at my paranoia. I knew that the People never shirked their work duties, but I knew, also, that Taras wasn't going to take no for an answer.

He was watching me, perhaps sensing my hesitation.

"How about lunch instead?" he suggested.

I nodded. It sounded like a good compromise. Everyone went back to eating, but I wasn't hungry anymore. I had too many butterflies in my stomach to make room for any more food. I excused myself from the table and forced myself to get ready calmly in my borrowed bedroom.

I tied my hair back with a piece of leather, and washed my face with the bowl of water that was beside my bed. I wound a piece of fabric around my finger and gave my teeth a scrub. I had seen how many of the older women in the village had lost their teeth, and I didn't ever want to join that number.

I found Nanaj waiting at the door, and followed her in self-conscious silence as she led me to the very back of the village. She hadn't reacted when her brother had asked me for lunch.

Maybe it only seems odd to me, I thought.

I decided not to ask.

"We're here," Nanaj told me, and she gestured to a door that was twice as wide as any of the others I had seen.

I followed her inside, where we were greeted by several women my own age, and two younger girls. The room was long and narrow, and lined on one side by tables, and on the other by an in-ground, low-burning fire.

I looked around in awed interest.

Small buckets were suspended over the fire, and as I watched, one of the women used a hook-like device to lift one of them down, then replaced it with another one.

The two younger girls grabbed the bucket and took it outside, waving to us as they went.

"This is the thaw room," Nanaj explained. "I'll show you the picking room and the growing room, too."

I followed her again, and she pushed aside a leather curtain at the end of the thaw room. It was icy cold, and dark. But when my eyes adjusted, I realized that it was bigger than it appeared, and that it was full of large baskets of root vegetables. Whitish carrots, large potatoes, and something that I thought might be a beet.

Nanaj grabbed onto my hand, and I let her lead me to another leather curtain. She opened it, and I blinked in confusion. The room was very nearly warm, and the air was almost thick. It smelled earthy and good.

There were rows and rows of dirt, and I frowned down at them, confused.

Nanaj fiddled with something on one of the walls, and suddenly a torch-fire lit the room. I gave her an envious look. During my fire-making lesson, it had taken me twenty minutes to get just a tiny spark.

She smiled at me, lifted the torch higher, and pointed up.

I looked toward the ceiling, and my eyes widened. Orange light reflected back at me, dancing across a shiny surface.

"What is it?" I asked.

"Ice," Nanaj replied, making it sound like the most obvious thing in the world.

I felt dazzled as I clued in. This strange room was a greenhouse.

I pictured it in the summer. Sun – cold, unforgiving, and present for up to twenty-four hours in a day – would be filtered through the polished sheets of ice, becoming concentrated and then heating the air and the ground beneath. It was a sophisticated system.

And it was further proof that Lanka and the People did not have any connection to the rest of the world. A highly specific farming system like this would've take taken years – no, *generations* – to perfect.

"Okay. Now we need to work," Nanaj told me.

She doused the torch in a bucket and guided me back to the room where the other women had already started.

There, they showed me how to break apart the frozen vegetables in the storage room, and how to thaw them over the fire. Each time a bucket was ready, a pair of the younger girls would run it out to one of the waiting families.

"Do you do this every day?" I asked.

"Less often during the growing season," Nanaj told me. "It's easy work. And we finish early. At lunch time. We'll pack up in just a moment."

As if on cue, Taras appeared in the doorway.

"Am I too early?" he asked.

"For what?" one of the women replied.

Taras turned his hawk-like gaze toward me, and a couple of the women laughed.

"I think you can take her," one of them said.

I blushed and looked down at my hands. They were dirty from digging through the vegetables. Nanaj handed me a cloth, and I wiped them off self-consciously.

"Have fun," she whispered. "And don't let him boss you around."

"Let's go," Taras said.

He helped me into my coat, took me by my good hand, and led me outside. He didn't let me go as we walked through town, and he chatted easily about the upcoming summer, about the gathering expedition he'd just come from, and about how big Andrik got each time he went away.

"Do you go away often?" I asked.

He looked down at me as if he was surprised that I didn't know.

"There is always something that must be done somewhere else," he told me, and it sounded like a quote.

Taras switched topics quickly, and began asking me probing questions about my life back home once again. At first, I tried to give him as little information as possible, but it was hard. There really was something about the way he asked questions that made me want to answer.

"Your house," he said. "It is made entirely of wood?"

"Mostly," I replied with a shrug.

It was about the third time he'd asked me, as though he expected to catch me in lie.

And his rapid-fire questions never seemed to stop.

In my world, I thought, *Taras would be a high-powered lawyer.*

"And you have a bathhouse within your made-of-wood home?"

"It's not a bathhouse," I corrected. "It is just a bath."

"Of your own?"

I laughed.

I had never before thought of my life as decadent, but all of the things I took for granted seemed downright luxurious when I discussed them with Taras.

I watched his face as he talked. It was animated and thoughtful. Lanka was so right. Her son was a very good-looking man.

He stopped at the edge of the village, stretched his arms above his head and flashed me a grin.

"Do you feel like an adventure?" he asked.

His eyes were almost devious, and I changed my mind suddenly. He wouldn't be a lawyer. He'd be a model.

Maybe an underwear model.

I blushed furiously as I immediately pictured Taras in a pair of snug boxer-briefs.

"Amazing," he said. "The colour of your cheeks is like the rising sun."

I felt the heat rise even more.

"Does no one here get embarrassed?" I blurted out.

Taras laughed, a deep baritone chuckle.

He placed his hands on my shoulders, and even through the padding that made up his mittens and my parka, I imagined that I could feel the warmth of them on my skin. He looked down at me with a curled-lip smile. He didn't try to pull me closer. Instead, he leaned in and pressed his lips against mine, ever so gently.

I froze.

Taras pushed a little harder – exploratory rather than aggressive. He moved, almost imperceptibly, and both of his lips closed around my bottom one. He pulled, ever so slightly, and I felt the blood rush down to my mouth. I brought my good hand up to rest on Taras's waist.

It was an odd position to be in. Two feet apart, yet locked in an intimate embrace.

He pulled away first.

"Better," Taras said.

"Better than what?"

"Better than when you try to pull away."

"I don't pull away," I protested.

He smiled like he knew better.

"I'm just not looking for a – " I cut myself off.

"For a what?" Taras prodded.

I didn't know what to say.

Another Ben, was what I had been thinking, and it surprised me.

Taras was nothing like Ben. Not that I could see, anyway. So where did the thought come from?

"Perhaps we should save the adventure for another day," he said softly, interrupting my worry. "Let's have lunch. I've got something prepared at home."

I swallowed hard and followed him to his house with a face that was probably red like a cherry, rather than red like the rising sun.

When we got inside, Taras laid out the food confidently, and waited until I'd tasted it and expressed my appreciation before he sat down himself. It was a mixture of fresh berries and something that had the texture of porridge.

"Thank you," I said shyly as he filled my bowl for the second time.

He ate a third, and then a fourth bowl, as I finished up my second one.

"I'll be back in a moment," he said, and jumped up.

I wondered suddenly if the People had rules about unmarried men and women spending time alone together.

I wished that I had thought to ask Nanaj.

But maybe Taras was above the rules anyway.

He came back to the table, and I noticed that he had changed into linen shorts and a sleeveless tunic.

Slipped into something more comfortable.

He stretched out on the ground, propping his head up with one of the floor pillows. His body was long, and well-muscled, and I had a hard time not staring at him. If he was at all self-conscious about his semi-exposed state, he didn't show it.

"With as much time as I spend travelling, I feel most comfortable in sleep clothes," he told me apologetically.

"You'd love flannel," I teased.

"Flannel?"

"It's like your linen fabric, but as soft as fur. My, um, sleep clothes at home are made from it."

He smiled. "I like it when you talk about things from your homeland."

"Why?"

"It's intriguing. Like you are." And then he added a word that I hadn't heard before.

"What's that one mean?" I asked.

"Interesting and far away," he replied.

I made the English translation.

Exotic.

I flushed.

"I could stay with you all day, talking like this," Taras told me.

"It's nice," I agreed.

"It would be nicer if you joined me down here," he added.

My face went red again, and he smiled.

"You are quite lovely, Lin-zee."

"Thank you."

He closed his eyes with a smile.

"Would you *like* to lie here?" he asked.

It sounded more like he'd already decided that I did want to, and was just being polite about asking me. I looked at him questioningly, trying to think of a good reason *not* to lie down beside him. He stretched his arms over his head, and I swallowed the nervous lump in my throat.

"With me," Taras added.

I'm over-thinking this, I told myself, and took a breath.

My face was flaming, and I was glad that his eyes were still closed. I jumped up from my seat, nearly knocking over the leftover lunch. I placed my pillow beside his, and made myself lie there, careful not to touch him.

He sighed, and reached over to caress my arm. My body shivered from the touch.

"Am I cold?" he asked.

"No," I whispered.

"Do I make you scared?"

"No."

"Hmm."

He sounded like he doubted me, but it was true. Mostly. There was something so deliberate about everything that Taras did that it was hard to imagine him doing anything dangerous or unpredictable.

If it had been Gavril, on the other hand...That man was the most unpredictable person I had ever met.

I steered my thoughts away, trying to focus on Taras.

"Is there somewhere you'd rather be?" Taras asked.

"No."

What was it with him and the direct questions?

He touched each of my eyelids, forcing them closed. I heard him shuffle a little, and then I felt his hand make a trail along my face. He kissed my forehead, and my cheeks, and my chin. He brushed his fingers along my lips, and I held very still.

It felt odd.

Nice, too.

But strange to be touched so intimately by a man who wasn't Ben.

My chest tightened as I thought of my former fiancé, and I tried to push aside the feeling.

It was hard, and I wondered if I should *tell* Taras about Ben.

Then I remembered a conversation I had overheard many years ago when I was waiting tables in an Italian restaurant.

Two young women had been sitting at a table together, whispering over their tiramisu while their third companion was in the bathroom.

"Can you believe it?" the blonde one had said.

The brunette shook her head. "I know. Who breaks off an engagement? Might as well have put a sign on her forehead."

"She's always going to be known as Gabby, the girl with the cold feet. She'll never snag another man now." The blonde glanced up and then shushed her friend. "Quiet. She's coming back."

A petite redhead with a Farrah Fawcett hairdo joined them.

"Oh, Gabs," the brunette sighed. "Have you been crying? Don't worry. The right man will come along eventually."

Would Taras care that I had been engaged? Did it matter if he did? I could almost hear Sadie, urging me to take advantage of the opportunity to kiss away the last bit of regret left over from my break-up with Ben.

What about Gavril? added my nagging internal voice.

What about him? I answered myself. *What does he have to do with anything?*

I commanded the voice to shut up, and I tipped my head back, further exposing my neck. Taras placed a kiss there, and it made me tingle again, just a bit. I let him trace his knuckles along my collarbone. It wasn't uncomfortable, or even unpleasant.

He rolled over abruptly, and neither of us made any move to get up.

We were both silent for several minutes.

"I should go," I said at last.

"I've crossed a line," Taras stated.

"No, that's not it."

At least not from my perspective, I added silently.

But I didn't know where the line was for the People.

"I sense your hesitation," Taras told me.

I struggled to find an appropriate response.

"I don't want to pressure you," he said. "I would never ask you to do anything you didn't feel comfortable doing."

I almost laughed. He sounded so much like a teenager during a make-out session.

"I want you to want me." Taras said it plainly, and directly, and it didn't sound cheesy at all.

"I don't feel pressured," I replied.

"I know that I've asked you before, but do you have a husband, in your homeland?" he asked.

"No. I wouldn't be here with you if I did."

"Is it Gavril?"

I felt my face go pink. "No."

"I've seen the way he looks at you."

How is that? I wondered, but I just shook my head.

"I would understand it," Taras added. "He did save your life."

"Reluctantly," I muttered in English.

Taras touched my cheek again. "What do you fear?"

There wasn't an easy answer. I feared the growing attachment I was forming to people in the village. I feared building a relationship that would have to be broken as soon as I got rescued.

If I ever do, I added reluctantly.

"I'm not afraid," I lied.

Taras looked thoughtful.

"Thank you for lunch," I added awkwardly.

We continued to lie on the floor.

"Do you want me to walk you to Gavril's house?" Taras asked.

I winced, thinking of Gavril and the anger he'd expressed when his brother had taken me out at night.

Where is he, anyway? I wondered.

"I'll be okay," I said at last.

Taras looked at me like he was going to argue, but he just shrugged, then helped me up.

"I'll walk with you again tomorrow," he promised. "And each day after that where the time allows. I'm a patient man, Lin-zee, when something is worth waiting for."

Then he gave me one of his signature feather-light kisses, and he let me leave.

***

Taras made good on his promise to walk with me every day that he could, and I knew that the People were noticing. When he wasn't around, they fed me tidbits of information about him.

"His favourite food is fried fish," one of them told me. "Most of the men like it baked because it stays soft. But Taras prefers it crispy."

"He can lift a reindeer over his head," another said in an awe-filled voice.

Nanaj had heard that one and grinned.

"He can *not* lift a reindeer over his head," she had corrected. "Just to his waist. But he can carry it the length of the village."

The attention made me feel self-conscious each time we walked together. I tried to keep my head lowered, but I knew that my blonde hair and awkward gait in the snow gave me away every time.

"Are you all right?" Taras asked one evening.

"Fine."

"How's your hand?"

"Almost perfect. Aside from the missing bits."

"Are you too tired to walk?" he wanted to know.

"No," I said truthfully.

I was still working with Nanaj and the others each morning, so my afternoons were my own, and I'd been going to sleep early every night.

I'd been staying in bed, too much, actually. Tiptoeing around Gavril was a full-time job. He'd finally started spending time at home, and he wasn't being very friendly.

He glowered at me each time he saw me, snapped at me when I mispronounced a word or even if I offered to help with the cooking. And I was doing my best to take it meekly. But I wasn't going to explain any of that to Taras.

"We have a long walk today," he warned, pointing to the pack on his back.

"All right," I agreed, and he grinned.

We set out at a quick pace, but before long, the terrain became a rocky tundra. I stumbled a few times, and Taras took my hand, wordlessly helping me along. I wished I could move as effortlessly as he could, but instead I was getting increasingly sweaty, and my breath was becoming laboured.

Are we there yet? I wanted to ask. *How many more minutes?*

At last we reached a wide hill. Taras led me to the top.

"Here," he said triumphantly.

He pulled his bag off his shoulder, set it on the ground, and began rummaging through it. He pulled out a leather-backed, woven mat, and a fur blanket. He laid the matt down on the ground.

"Sit," he suggested.

Once I'd complied, he wrapped the blanket around my shoulders and went back to digging through his pack.

"Are you hungry?" he asked.

"Sure," I agreed, though my stomach was actually tossing and turning nervously.

Taras hadn't tried to kiss me on any of our public walks, and he hadn't taken me back to his house again, either. In fact, this was the first time we'd been really alone since we had lunch together. And it was making me feel jumpy.

Taras produced a package wrapped in wax-lined linen.

"Sandwiches," he told me, his tongue forming the English word awkwardly.

I stared at him in disbelief as he sat down beside me.

"Sandwiches?"

"Andrik told me that at home, your favourite thing to do was something called a picnic and I thought that you might miss it," he explained. "We don't make sandwiches here, but it seemed like an easy thing."

I unwrapped the linen, and sure enough, it contained two slabs of unleavened bread filled with salted meat. I picked one up and took a big bite.

"How is it?" Taras asked.

"Needs mayonnaise," I joked in English.

"What?" He looked puzzled, and I laughed.

"It's perfect," I amended.

"Good."

Taras ate his, and also finished the other half of mine. When he was done, he slid his hand underneath the blanket and pulled the mitten off my good hand so that he could weave his fingers through mine.

"Watch the horizon," he said.

I stared at its greyness intently. I saw nothing.

"Give it a moment," Taras suggested, sensing my impatience.

I waited, still staring, and inhaled sharply as a glimmer appeared in the sky.

A bluish thread of light danced across my vision, ebbing and flowing, and brightening to a brilliant green. It spread out like a curtain, and I couldn't tear my gaze away.

"This is the colour of your eyes," Taras murmured in my ear.

His soft exhale against my cheek made me warm. I wanted to turn my head, just to see if our lips would meet. But the lights above wouldn't let me move.

"Keep watching," he said unnecessarily.

For about fifteen brilliant minutes, the Northern Lights lit the edge of the sky. And then they faded to purple, and clouds overtook the position.

"Thank you," I breathed.

He stroked my arm under the blanket, and I leaned into the touch.

"It won't be long before I have to leave the village again," he told me.

"Where will you go?" I asked.

"Guard duty," he replied easily.

I thought of the men who seemed to be watching over the village the night that Taras sneaked me out of Nanaj's house. Was there actually something to fear? I'd very nearly forgotten Lanka's warning about not being alone.

"What are you guarding?" I wanted to know.

"The People," he said.

"Against what?"

He stiffened, ever so slightly, and I stifled a sigh. For all of Lanka's insistence that I become a part of the village, I still felt like I was missing something.

"I'll be gone for quite some time. Longer than when we went for the hunt." Taras's answer to my inquiry was effortlessly evasive.

"Okay."

"I lead them out just before the sun makes its first ascent of the season," he added. "I would have liked to have shown you that, as well. But when we return, it will already be getting dark again."

"I wonder if I'll still be here then," I said thoughtfully.

Taras frowned. "Where else would you be?"

"Home?"

He leaned in then, held my face tightly between his hands, and kissed me with a sense of ownership that surprised me.

"Hey," I said softly when I finally pulled away.

"I would prefer it if you were still here," he told me.

I didn't reply to that comment. I felt claustrophobic suddenly, in spite of the open space. I leaned away slightly, afraid to make eye contact.

"Wouldn't you miss me, if you left? And doesn't it make you sad that I'm going?" he asked after a moment.

The questions surprised me, mostly because they seemed out of sync with his confident personality and smooth comments. But I didn't have to think about my answer.

"Yes," I admitted.

"Good," he replied.

Something about the way Taras said it made me look more closely at his face. He was smiling a small, self-satisfied smile, and I realized that he hadn't asked the question for reassurance. He had wanted to make sure that *I* knew that I would miss him. As if it would make me stay.

"I have something to tell you," Taras said.

"Okay."

Taras put his hand on his chin thoughtfully. "Will it make you uncomfortable?"

"Why would it?" I wondered out loud.

"Do you remember the story I told, about Pala?"

I nodded.

"There's more to it than I shared on that night."

"All right."

For some reason, my stomach was starting to churn.

"Ria's prophecy contained a very specific description of the foretold leader's wife. She said that the wife will be a stranger among us, and that this stranger will help to change the People's course. The story also says that this stranger will be a beautiful woman, or a kind woman. Or both. She will blend seamlessly with the People, and she will actually *draw out* Pala's successor. The exact words of the story state that she will be like a bright, colourful stitch in a beautiful blanket."

"Okay," I said again.

He smiled. "This has always made me think of the patterned beadwork that Lanka does on her quilts. Unique. Stunning. And impossible to recreate."

I immediately thought of the drape hanging in front of Gavril's bedroom, and I flushed guiltily. Even with all my politeness, he'd been crankier than ever toward me this morning. He'd shouted at me when I dropped a bowl, and had stomped out angrily.

I was at a loss. I didn't know how to fix the awkwardness between us.

I realized that Taras was watching my face.

"Is something wrong?" he asked.

"I'm fine," I answered.

"Do you see where I'm going with this story?"

"No."

But then I did see.

"No," I repeated, this time more emphatically.

"We don't get strangers in the village," Taras told me.

"It's just a story."

He shook his head. "Lin-zee. It's not just a story. It is *the* story."

The intensity of Taras's words unsettled me. They were filled with religious fervour.

"Before Pala became ruler, our prophecy was a different one. It foretold of Pala and Ria themselves, and how they would shape our People. It said that a man of indescribable wisdom and a woman of incredible foresight would both unite and divide the People. And before that, it was a story about a powerful man named Kol and his wife, Innis. Every few generations, the prophecy comes to fruition. And once it's passed, a new story is foretold. It has been this way for as long as the People have existed."

I stared at Taras, unsure what to say. His gaze relaxed just a little, and he stroked my face gently.

"I felt that I should tell you more, since I'm leaving. The People have a rich tradition of storytelling, and all of it has meaning. It's tied to our very being."

"Taras, this isn't a story about me," I protested. "I'm hardly blending seamlessly."

A gust of wind cut through the air, and I shivered.

See? I wanted to say. *The slightest breeze and I'm freezing. I don't fit in here at all.*

Taras pulled me closer.

"I may have left another thing out of the story," he admitted softly.

"What's that?"

"This beautiful woman is said to have a defect, like Ria, Pala's wife."

That sounds more like me, I thought wryly.

Taras nodded, smiling at my expression.

"This defect is a specific one. It is said that the stranger will have one lame hand," he explained. "She will only be made whole through virtue of her marriage to the leader of our People."

Taras met my eyes, and there was a question there that I didn't want to answer. I shivered again, and this time it wasn't because of the cold. I clenched my injured hand into a malformed fist. I couldn't make myself meet Taras's eyes.

"Come on," he said abruptly. "It's going to storm."

***

Within minutes, the snow was coming down hard, and I had to hold on to Taras for nearly the whole trek back to the village. He walked me as far as Gavril's door.

"I have to go," he said regretfully. "They'll be expecting me to help."

"Okay," I agreed.

I was exhausted, both physically and emotionally. But when I entered the house and found Gavril himself sitting at the large table in the eating area, I felt compelled to be polite.

"Hello," I said.

He grunted.

My tiredness made me irritable, and I was unreasonably annoyed about his behaviour over the past few days. In fact, I was still annoyed that he'd yanked me away from Taras, and that had happened more than a week ago.

I unbuttoned my coat and tossed it haphazardly onto one of the hooks.

"I said hello," I snapped as I sat down beside him Gavril looked up at me in surprise.

"Why are you so angry at me?" I demanded.

He went wide-eyed, but still said nothing.

"I don't know why you're staring at me like that," I almost shouted.

I knew it was a lie before the whole sentence was even out of my mouth. I did know. I'd been going out of my way to accommodate Gavril's temper since he'd come home from the gathering expedition. And the problem wasn't him, it was me.

And it was the reason for my careful behaviour.

Good, old-fashioned guilt.

I'd believed that this man, who had saved my life, was an abusive husband. Then I'd refused to rest when he'd told me to, and I'd been spending all of my free time with his brother, whom he clearly disliked.

I cringed inwardly.

"I'm sorry," I said.

I stood up again, preparing to grab my parka.

"Where are you going?" Gavril asked in a too-quiet voice.

I ignored him, and began to slip my boots back onto my feet. I didn't have anywhere else to go, of course.

"Are you going back to see Taras?" he demanded. "Is that your plan?"

"Why do you care?" I retorted.

"I *don't* care!" he shouted.

We stared at each other.

"Please, sit," he finally said, sounding strained.

"Fine."

"I apologize for my outburst," he said formally.

"That's a first," I replied sarcastically, but my heart wasn't in it.

"I think that you should know that Taras was to be married once before." He said it without looking at me.

"So? So was I."

Gavril smiled just a little bit. "Does Taras know that?"

"I don't see why it's his business."

Gavril laughed.

"You have an odd sense of humour," I told him.

"I think many things are funny," he informed me. "I thought it was very funny when you bit Lanka."

"*Tried* to bite her," I corrected.

He laughed again, deep and low. A bass to Taras's baritone.

Gavril reached out and touched my damaged hand. It was bandaged lightly, just enough to protect the new skin.

"You should still be changing this twice a day," he said.

"My doctor must have forgotten to tell me that," I replied.

He slid just a little closer and began unwrapping the bandages.

I watched him silently, noticing again how sure and gentle his hands were. The movements were so at odds with his bristly personality.

He finished removing the wrappings and explored the ridges of my amputation with the tips of his fingers. He lingered briefly where my pinky used to be, then slid his hand along my wrist.

"Your presence frightens me," he said without looking up. "It brings a change. This is something which my brother not only welcomes, but demands. But me…It's a change that I don't desire."

"I'm sorry," I said helplessly.

"Yes."

"You could have left me out in the snow to die," I reminded him, but my words didn't have any heat.

"I saw the flash in the sky and I knew," Gavril told me. "I've never been more frightened in my life. And yet I knew what I would find."

"What's that?"

"You."

He brought his gaze up to my face, and I felt my breath catch. His eyes were full of warmth, and as far from being clinically detached as they could be.

"Lindsay," he said my name slowly.

"Please, Gavril."

His hand moved from my wrist to my waist, and then he pulled me against him, crushing me against his chest, just the way I'd imagined. And I wasn't going to let the chance slip away.

I tipped my face up, and stood on my toes so I could press my lips gently onto his. I heard him draw in a breath, and then he was kissing me fiercely. I responded without hesitation. He paused and pulled away, just for a second, and I threw myself at him. Literally.

He collapsed backwards, exposing the tender skin between his collarbone and his chin.

I ran my mouth along his throat gently, and then along his jaw. My lips met with dark stubble, and the roughness made my mouth ache pleasantly. His hands slid over my back and down my hips, leaving a trail of undeniable desire in their wake.

"Gavril."

I could barely form his name.

He rolled me over, and slipped his fingers under my shirt.

Oh god.

I burned with the feel of his skin on my skin. His hand crawled up, up, and he cupped one breast tenderly, and I moaned. I shifted a little to give him better access. I willed him to take it further.

This is what you've been missing, said a small voice in my head.

I didn't know exactly what it meant, but in spite of that, I knew the self-directed statement was true.

"Gavril," I repeated.

And without warning, he tore himself away from me.

I trembled, startled by the sudden loss.

"Taras," he said in a rough voice.

He was the furthest thing from my mind.

Gavril stood up, and gazed down at me with a defeated expression on his face.

"I can't," he whispered.

"Please," I was begging, and I didn't care.

"I will send Lanka," he told me.

"I don't want Lanka," I replied.

Gavril grabbed his parka and tossed it on without buttoning it up. His face was hard.

"There's a storm out there," I reminded him.

He glanced at me, and his eyes softened. He stepped toward me, buttoning his coat as he came. He looked, for just a second, like he was going to kiss me again, but he just touched my cheek, then turned on his heel and fled.

I drew my knees up to my chin, and cried into them. I felt drained. And even more guilty than I had before.

And Lanka was on her way.

I started to stand up, determined to climb into bed before she arrived. I didn't want to have to explain my tears. But I wasn't quite quick enough. She came bursting through the door before I could even finish getting to my feet.

"My son says that I must speak with you," she informed me resentfully. "He commanded it."

She threw her coat on top of mine.

"Sorry for the inconvenience," I muttered half-heartedly in English.

Lanka frowned. "I've told you before, if you wish to communicate, you must speak in the People's language."

"I wish to communicate," I replied. "But I do *not* wish to lose myself."

"Hmm."

I ignored her disbelieving look. "What did Gavril want you to say to me?"

"Gavril?"

"Yes."

"It was Taras who required me to speak with you."

My skin got hot. "Taras?"

"Hmm," she said again, and took a step back.

She examined my face as if noticing my expression – one part blotchy and one part flushed – and my slightly dishevelled appearance for the first time.

I pretended not to notice her scrutiny.

"Okay. What did *Taras* want?" I asked.

I didn't know if it made me feel slightly relieved, or if it made me even more worried that it was him, rather than Gavril, who wanted Lanka to speak with me.

"He informed you that he will be leaving?" she asked.

"For guard duty," I confirmed.

"He made it sound easy?"

I nodded.

Lanka sighed loudly. "I must explain something to you. On the other side of our land, there is another village."

I tensed, knowing that I was finally going to be let in on the secret.

"Taras and some others told a story on the night he and the other men returned from the hunt? In the lodge? Do you remember?" she asked.

I nodded again, afraid if I spoke she would change her mind about sharing whatever it was with me.

"I'm never sure they truly understand its significance," she said. "Didn't you wonder what happened to the two infants, the twin sons of Pala and Ria?"

"I had kind of forgotten, really," I admitted.

"Not surprising. I'm sure Taras put most of the focus on other parts of the story. He often forgets that Pala was a husband and a father first, and a leader second," Lanka told me.

I didn't tell her that he had put more than enough emphasis on the *husband* aspect.

"Pala felt that his sons were both his greatest accomplishment and his greatest failure. They symbolized the life that could have been, and the life would be, and it nearly ripped Pala in two. He tried to embrace the latter, but was often reminded of the former," Lanka continued. "And there were people who favoured once sentiment, or the other. Many supported Pala's initiative, and they wanted to make a life working with the weather, working with the land, and working with Pala himself. They mourned the loss of Ria, but they carried on. They saw a future. Sadly there were some who disagreed heartily with Pala's decisions – especially his choice to cast aside his role as ruler of the People. They felt that they had been robbed of a leader. And they weren't willing to sit by quietly to let Pala rob them of another. In the still of the night, during the long-awaited Thaw, they kidnapped the elder son – born just moments before his brother – and fled. Eventually they travelled farther than any of the People ever had before, and settled in the area we now call the growing region. They considered their good fortune to be a sign of their righteousness, and they named themselves the Outsiders, because they were no longer of the People, and never would be again. They were proud of it. Pala sent an envoy to negotiate the return of his son. They immediately killed the envoy. Then the Freeze came, and the tundra was once again impassable. As soon as the Thaw came a second time, Pala led an army to take his son back by force. But they were prepared for that, too, and defeated the army easily. Pala was forced to retreat. He began training a *new* army, but they weren't ready in time for the next Thaw, and the Outsiders came to the village instead. They were brutal in their attack, stealing children and food, and burning down houses. After this assault, Pala created the very first Guard. They are an elite group of men, who train year round to protect the People just one time each year. The Outsiders have never again broken through to the village."

"Just a few minor details," I murmured.

"Truly, the Outsiders used to be our People. Though the younger ones – including Taras – don't like it," Lanka said. "The Outsiders look much as we do. They speak much as we do. But that is where the similarities end. They lack the skills of the People. They do not grow food because they cannot grow it. They do not live in peace because they cannot live in peace. They fight amongst themselves, even over the most plentiful things. They would fight over snow if they could do it. And each year during the Thaw, they send a group of warriors to try to take back our land, though they have so much already. Each generation, we try to reason with them, to make them see that both of us may live here, with no need to fight. But they don't reason."

"That's terrible," I said.

"If the Outsiders would only ask we would gladly trade our resources for theirs. But they don't ask. They take and they take."

"What do they take?"

"Anything that's not tied to the ground. Supplies. Tools. Children."

I felt ill.

I knew I hadn't exactly crash landed in a war zone, but the worst kind of battle I'd ever witnessed had been on a paintball course.

"Do you have this kind of conflict where you live?" Lanka asked.

I shook my head.

"Not exactly where I live. But in other places, not so far away."

She nodded, satisfied by my answer. "Our men would choose not to fight, if they had the option. The Guard exists out of necessity – *perpetual* necessity."

"And Taras leads the Guard against the Outsiders?" I asked.

"Yes," Lanka agreed. "That is what he does. Our men are strong, and well-trained. They begin learning how to fight when they're young, and they never stop. The Outsiders are soft, and lazy. Their leadership never prepares them as we prepare our men. The Guard discourages as often as it fights."

"Do the Outsiders ever succeed?"

"Rarely."

"But occasionally?" I persisted.

"Yes. And even when we are successful, men sometimes die."

The position of the village and its layout suddenly made more sense to me. The mountains behind it assured that no one could attack from behind. The concentrated cluster of dwellings insured that the Guard could keep everyone safe at once if need be.

"And Taras wanted you to tell me all of this?" I asked.

"No," Lanka replied dismissively. "Taras wanted me to discuss marriage."

I swallowed. "He what?"

"He wishes to wed you."

I said nothing.

"You have no questions about this?"

"No," I lied.

Marriage? To me? We barely knew each other. Of course I had questions. I had a hundred questions. And a hundred arguments.

Lanka was staring at me disbelievingly again.

"Do I have the right to refuse?" I whispered, suddenly worried.

"Of course you do," she stated. "And I told Taras that he must wait."

"Wait for what?"

"I thought his time on the Guard might give you time to consider other options," she explained.

Gavril.

She knew, somehow. Maybe my face had given it away.

Lanka raised an eyebrow. "*I* have a question for *you*."

"Okay."

"Have you given any more thought to going home?"

"Every day," I started to say, and then stopped.

Because I'd stopped looking for planes in the sky. I was no longer concerned about going three days without a hot shower. I'd stopped wondering how my best friend would feel about each new food I tried. When I did mention leaving, it was because someone else had brought it up. I hadn't dreamed of peanut butter in... How long had it been? How long had I been in the village now?

"It's time," Lanka told me, and for a second I thought that she meant to send me packing.

My heart sagged, and judging from Lanka's expression, so did my face.

"For me to go," she amended. "Not you."

She smiled and touched my face in an affectionate gesture.

"Bye," I said in English.

"Goodnight," she replied in the People's language.

As she headed to bed, I realized suddenly that I was just as scared of leaving the Village as I was of being stuck there forever.

Chapter Ten

The storm lasted for two and a half days, and I was trapped in the house for the duration, while a flurry of activity went on in the blinding snow outside.

Taras came by once, just to let me know that the Guard was preparing to leave, snow or not, and every capable body had a role to play. Everyone except me.

Of course, I couldn't see in the white out, and I could barely make my way around using the ropes that connected the village. I had no skill in making or maintaining weapons, and I had no experience preparing the kinds of food that would sustain the men in their crusade. So instead, I sat in Gavril's house, waiting, and feeling on edge.

I made food for myself and for Lanka if she was there. Gavril never seemed to come home. Lanka had explained to me that he was one of the few men who didn't join the Guard. The village was too worried about losing their healer to allow him to go. And the few times I *did* see him, he was detachedly polite, and he didn't mention our encounter.

But I couldn't erase it from my mind. It was sealed inside me. And not just in my memory, either. My whole body remembered him at varying parts every day. I would touch something with my hand, and think of his rough one. I'd catch myself running my fingers over my stomach, aching as I recalled the way he'd done the same.

I felt ignored. But self-centred. And sleep was even more fitful than usual.

Which is why, on the third night of the storm, I wasn't expecting to be needed, and I was trying – without much success – to get back to sleep. I'd woken up just moments earlier, but it was the third time that night. My stomach was twisted with guilt, and I'd been unsure why until I'd come to just then, gasping against cold air that wasn't there.

I'd been dreaming of snow, and of Anna again, and her two students.

What were their names? Why *couldn't I remember?*

It was terrible that I couldn't. I was the last person to see them alive. The last person to speak to them. And somewhere, someone was missing them. Waking up in the morning like I just had, wondering if they'd suffered.

They had husbands. They'd talked about them. That I remembered. Had they had children? Even if they hadn't, what about their other family? Their friends? Tears built up in my eyes.

Survivor's guilt, I acknowledged.

I wasn't sure why I hadn't experienced it with such force any sooner. Maybe I'd been too busy with trying to find a way off the People's island to consider it. Or maybe the feeling had been there all along, and I'd been ignoring it. And now that I had stopped thinking about getting home – and I had some time to myself – I was ready to confront it.

I shivered, even though I was quite warm. I would probably never find out what had happened to the other passengers on the plane or to the pilot. I didn't even know if the rest of the plane had crashed anywhere near my lone seat. I felt pained by that fact, and when I inhaled deeply, I realized that I was crying.

Then I felt a hand on my arm, and I realized that Gavril was in my bedroom.

"What?" I said, hoping that the catch in my voice would be mistaken for sleepiness.

Gavril shook my shoulder, a little too insistently.

"I need your help," he told me stiffly.

"*My* help?"

"There is no one else," he replied.

His tone almost made me refuse, but there was something in his eyes that made me sit up instead.

"There's a hundred other people who could help," I said a little sullenly.

"The Guard has gone," he informed me.

"Oh."

Taras had left without saying good-bye. For some reason I wasn't surprised.

"Will you help?" Gavril asked.

"Where's Lanka?" I wanted to know.

He made an exasperated noise. "She was needed elsewhere."

I sighed. "I'm getting up."

Gavril turned away, but didn't leave the room as I got dressed.

I followed him through the hallway, complaining all the way. When we reached the front door, I went silent in surprise.

A man I didn't recognize was waiting by the flap with a nervous expression on his face. He held an oil lamp and kept shifting from foot to foot. He hadn't removed his parka, and it was dirty and ripped. He seemed oblivious to the snow that was melting off his body and forming a pool at his feet. When he saw me, his eyes went a little wild.

"Gavril, you said you were going to get help!" His voice was gravelly, and innately angry.

"Shut up," Gavril replied.

I blinked in surprise. Gavril was always cranky but he wasn't usually so...mean.

He handed me my jacket, and once I was bundled into it, he tethered me to his own parka.

"Let's go," he said.

We headed out into the blinding white.

It was the first time I'd seen it since the light flurry had started days earlier. Even though I was tied to Gavril securely, and even though I knew that he must be using the ropes between the buildings, the oppressive snow storm filled me with panic. It reminded me too much of the plane crash. My hand throbbed with remembered pain.

Gavril was moving quickly, urgently, without checking to see if I was keeping up. For one terrible second, the tether between us went slack. I couldn't see him in front of me, or feel him. I tried to yell, but the wind whipped my voice away.

I took a shaky step forward, and crashed with relicf into Gavril's thick form. I wrapped myself around one of his arms, and I didn't let go until we reached our destination.

Gavril didn't waste any time getting us into the dwelling, and as we entered, I realized we were in Nanaj's house. Gavril helped me take my coat off and turned to the unknown man.

"Where is she?" he demanded.

The man didn't answer immediately.

"Elak!" Gavril shouted. "Where is Nanaj?"

My eyes snapped up, making the connection. This was the husband who had caused my friend such harm. The man whom Lanka disapproved of, and the one whom Taras had sent away, just a few days earlier. What was he doing there?

"Nanaj is in the bedroom," Elak finally replied.

"Come," Gavril ordered.

I followed closely behind him as he marched down Nanaj's hallway. I wanted to keep some space between myself and Elak.

Nanaj was lying on her bed, drenched in sweat and breathing hard. Her face was a mottled purple, and I thought that I could smell blood.

She smiled tiredly at me. "Lin-zee. Thank you for coming."

"No problem," I said softly.

Gavril gave her a quick but thorough once over.

"The baby is coming," he told us in a tight voice.

"Is it too early?" I whispered.

Gavril nodded curtly.

Nanaj groaned.

"Elak!" Gavril shouted. "Elak!"

The other man appeared at the bedroom door, looking nervous. He stepped inside warily, and looked anywhere but at his wife.

"What did you do to her?" Gavril demanded. "Tell me."

Elak eyes dropped to the floor, and he said something unintelligible.

"Louder," Gavril commanded.

"I just wanted to talk."

"Did Taras lift your ban?"

Elak shook his head.

Nanaj whimpered, and I turned my attention to her. I sat down beside her bed, tuning the men out, and trying to remember everything I could about being a labour coach. I had helped Sadie through two births, but it seemed like a lifetime ago.

"Breathe," I said. "In through your nose and out through your mouth. You can do this."

"She is my *wife*!" Elak shouted suddenly.

I looked up just in time to see him shove Gavril.

Gavril stumbled backwards momentarily before righting himself and squaring off to face the other man.

"She *was* your wife," he corrected in a soft and cold voice. "As the eldest son of Yuri, eldest son of Borislav, I declare that she is yours no longer."

Elak's face drained of colour. He lunged, and at first I thought that he was going after Gavril again. But then I realized that Nanaj was his intended target. I braced myself, shifting to shield my friend's body.

But Gavril was quicker.

His meaty fist met the side of Elak's face, and with a sickening crack, the other man collapsed on the floor.

I looked from one to the other, stunned.

Gavril took my chin in his hand.

"The baby," he said. "I believe it is time to push."

"Yes," I replied faintly.

I refocused, and began giving Nanaj as much encouragement as I could muster. Even through my friend's grunts and shouts, it was hard to keep from checking to see if Elak had woken up.

"The head," Gavril said finally.

Seconds later, he held up a tiny baby boy, blue and unbreathing. He laid the child gently on the bed and said a string of words I didn't recognize.

Swear words, I realized.

I looked down at the tiny blue form. He was the smallest person I had ever seen.

Why wasn't he breathing?

I scooped him up and pressed my head to his chest. At first, I couldn't hear anything over the rush of blood in my own head. I tried to concentrate on the baby.

Yes. It was there. A tiny heartbeat.

"Breathe," I said.

I pressed my fingers gently into his chest, compressing what I hoped was the correct spot. Once. Twice. I tipped his tiny head back and exhaled softly into his mouth.

"Breathe," I said again.

I repeated the sequence. I knew that I had tears sliding down my face.

Compress, one, two. Exhale, one, two.

On the sixth try, the infant boy took a sputtering gasp on his own.

"Yes!" I shouted.

He inhaled again, and the blue tinge left his face. I picked him up and handed him to my friend. Both she and Gavril were staring at me.

"CPR," I told them in English.

Nanaj lifted her son to her breast, and the room was silent except for the occasional contented sigh from the baby.

"Nanaj," Gavril finally said without taking his eyes off me. "Do you object to having Norath, son of Darev, as your husband?"

"I do not," she replied.

"I will speak with Lanka," Gavril told her. "I believe that Norath will gladly make you his wife."

"And Elak?" Nanaj asked softly.

"Elak will need to catch up to the Guard when he wakes up. When he comes back, he may have this house, and live every day with his shame. You and the children can move in with Norath right away."

"Is it safe?" I interrupted. "To move Nanaj and the kids during the storm?"

"I believe that the storm has already passed," Gavril said.

I smiled tiredly at him, thinking that his words had a more metaphorical meaning than he knew.

Chapter Eleven

I had heard the term "uneasy truce" before, but had never personally experienced it until Gavril and I started working together.

With Taras and the Guard gone, there was a lot more manual labour to be done by those who were left behind, and therefore a lot more minor injuries to be tended to. I would never have pictured myself in the role of nursemaid, but after word got around that I had saved Nanaj's newborn son, it was assumed that I would be assisting Gavril on a more regular basis.

Each day, he and I ate breakfast together, then headed over to his infirmary. He was polite and never said a word about our pre-storm kiss. So I followed. Sometimes, the time we spent together was nearly enjoyable, and I would almost have called our uneasy truce something more. Something almost companionable.

One afternoon, Gavril left me alone in the shop to make a house call, and I found that I actually missed his bossy instructions.

"Don't go anywhere," he had commanded just before leaving. "Someone might need your help."

But that had been hours earlier, and not one patient had come through the door. I had examined the contents of all his jars, folded a big stack of linen bandages, and I was getting more bored by the second.

"iPod," I muttered to myself. "This is an iPod kind of day."

The rustle of the door flap stoked my irritation.

"You've got a lot of nerve!" I shouted.

I didn't know if the phrase translated properly or not, but I decided to take the chance. I put my hands on my hips, and stood in the middle of the room. I waited for him to come in, prepared with my tirade.

"I swear, if you ever—" I cut myself off.

It wasn't Gavril under the pile of fur-trimmed coat. It was Nanaj.

"Oh!" I said excitedly. "I'm so glad to see you! Sorry for shouting. I thought you were Gavril."

I hugged my friend enthusiastically. I hadn't seen her at all in the two weeks since the baby was born.

She grinned at me. "You yell at him?"

"Only when he deserves it. That surprises you?"

"It only surprises me that he would put up with it," she teased.

"He doesn't have a choice," I told her. "He wants my help here."

"I find that surprising, too."

"What?"

"That he wants help."

I smiled. "Maybe not so much *wants*. But he needs me. Gavril is a very competent healer. But his bedside manner is seriously lacking."

"You sound as though you're starting to like him."

I blushed. "He's a pain, but he could be worse."

Nanaj laughed. "He was going to give me some more salve for my eye."

I winced. Her bruises had faded, and the cuts on her face were looking better, but the evidence Elak had left behind was still highly visible. I went to the shelf and dug through the jars until I found the one that would help my friend.

"How's the baby?" I wanted to know.

"Good. Lanka's watching him while he naps. You should come by today to see him. You can stay for lunch," she suggested.

"Okay. I'd like that."

We both turned at the sound of the door flap opening. Gavril gave me a tight-lipped smile and nodded at his sister as he came in.

"I'll leave you alone," Nanaj whispered. "So that you can shout at him."

"Thanks," I said wryly.

She slipped out and Gavril hung up his coat.

"Hello," I greeted.

He ignored me.

"How was the little boy's rash?" I asked.

He ignored me again.

What happened to our uneasy truce? I wondered.

"Gavril?"

"I've been to see Lanka," he informed me. "And the boy's rash has cleared."

I stood there staring at him. His back was to me, and his body was rigid. I could see the stiffness of his posture, even underneath his parka.

He finally spun to face me. "Are you going to accept his proposal?"

"What?"

"Will. You. Accept." He bit the words off, one by one.

Oh. Why had Lanka even told him?

"If you're referring to Taras, he hasn't asked me yet," I replied coldly.

It was an absurd response, and it was the least of my worries about my likelihood of marrying Gavril's brother. I had far greater things to think about. Like the fact that in a village full of people who had known each other since birth, Taras and I were nearly strangers. Or that accepting a marriage proposal was tantamount to accepting that I would never be going home. And then there was the fact that Taras considered me to be the woman out of a local legend.

And even if none of *that* was true...Just a month and a half earlier, I'd run to the other side of the world to *avoid* getting married. Not to jump into a different one.

"Yet," Gavril stated. "So you know that he will."

"I don't know anything but what Lanka told me," I retorted. "And I don't see why it matters to you, anyway."

"And when he does ask?" Gavril persisted. "What then?"

"I don't know," I replied evenly.

How can you not know? I asked myself.

Gavril wasn't going to let it go, either. "Do you know what it means, to marry Taras?"

"The usual, I would think."

"It's a lifetime commitment. The People don't take marriage lightly."

"Neither do I."

"And with Taras..."

"What?"

"It will be a commitment of lifetimes to come, if he has his way. He wants to cement his role as leader and..." Gavril ran his fingers through his hair irritably.

"And what?"

"Has he even invited you into his home?"

I couldn't make sense of his thought process.

"What does that have to do with anything?" I sounded as exasperated as I felt.

"It's just a question," Gavril said. "Does it not strike you as odd that he didn't ask you to become his guest rather than mine?"

"You didn't exactly invite me in with open arms, either," I retorted.

"You have never been unwelcome here," Gavril said, but it sounded strained. "I didn't realize you felt forced upon me."

"How else could I feel?"

He didn't answer.

"Would it be easier if I left?" I asked.

"No!"

The force of his answer surprised me.

"Then ask me to stay," I suggested.

He stared me down with a pain-filled glare.

"What am I missing?" I asked.

"I can't," he said.

"Can't what? Ask me to stay?"

Again, he didn't answer.

"Why did you kiss me?" I asked softly.

"*You* kissed *me*," he replied.

My face went hot. Was that how it had happened? It hadn't seemed so one-sided at the time.

"You kissed me back," I said in a strangled whisper.

"I didn't mean to," he snapped. "I'm very sorry that I did."

I didn't know if I was embarrassed, or just plain angry. And I wasn't sticking around to find out.

"I'm going to go," I told him.

It was meant to sound like a threat, but it came out as a sign of defeat. I grabbed my parka and headed outside.

And Gavril made no move to stop me.

***

The sky was thick and grey, and the paths were lined with people taking advantage of the muted light. It was still cold, but I had been assured that before too long, the sun would make a real appearance and it would be warm enough to be outdoors with just a woven sweater.

I strode through the village, keeping my frustration with Gavril as well-hidden as I could manage.

But when I tripped over a loose piece of ice, it took all of my willpower to stop myself from kicking it angrily aside.

I stopped in front of Nanaj's new house. I stared at the door. A bridal wreath hung above it, announcing that a marriage had occurred recently.

I hesitated. I still hadn't mastered the concept that I could let myself into a neighbour's house whenever I felt like it, and I knew that once again, I was arriving much earlier than she probably expected.

"Hello there," said a voice from behind me.

I turned, and felt relieved to see Norath, Nanaj's new husband, looking at me from behind a pile of folded linens. He flicked his too-long hair back with a little toss of his head. His mouth sagged on one side, and his nose was crooked, but when he smiled, his whole face lit up. I hadn't met him officially, but his limping gait and distinctive features made him easy to recognize.

"Oh, good," I said. "May I come in?"

Norath's face nearly split in two with amusement. He nodded.

"Yes, please," he replied. "I'm just dropping off these diapers for Kalav, and then I am back to laundry duty. You can have her all to yourself. My wife."

He said the last word proudly. I'd learned that Norath had been twice rejected as a husband, and that he viewed his sudden acquisition of both a wife and a family as the most fortunate of circumstances.

"Thank you," I said gratefully, and held the tent flap open for him.

Inside, I could hear Nanaj chattering happily to her baby.

"Hello!" she called out as we came into the house.

I automatically scooped Kalav up from his bassinet. I buried my face in his sweet-smelling head, and let Nanaj and Norath have a moment to themselves. The baby yawned sleepily, and I smiled down at him.

"Who's a good boy?" I murmured.

"You should have children," Nanaj said from behind me.

I turned to her. Norath was already gone.

"Maybe one day," I replied.

She examined my face. "What's wrong?"

I sighed, and felt a pang of longing for Sadie. Nanaj was a friend, and I thought that we might one day be close, but Sadie was my *best* friend, and it had been so easy with her. I never had to worry about what I could or couldn't say. I wondered if she was missing me too. I mean, I knew that she must miss me as much as I missed her, but did she know yet that I was gone? Had she emailed me a hundred times and received no reply and become worried?

Email.

I almost laughed.

"Lin-zee?"

"I'm fine," I lied finally.

"I can tell that something is wrong."

"Does it bother you at all that Gavril chose a new husband for you?" I asked.

"No," she replied without hesitation.

"Not at all?"

"Elak and I weren't a good match. Lanka was correct to disapprove of our marriage. I was foolish to ignore her request. You know, Elak and I had to live on the mountainside for many months, alone. In a cave!" She laughed at the last statement. "When I became pregnant with Andrik, we came home, but only because I begged him to. It was then that he began to hit me. It stopped for a while when Andrik was born, but it didn't take long for it to start up again. This kind of behaviour isn't usually tolerated by the People, and at first I hid what was happening. Elak's time on the Guard kept him away, and he was careful to restrain himself in front of our son. But my mother found out, and she did her best to enforce our laws. She banned him from the village, twice, but he came back both times. And then Taras found out, too, and banned him once again. He came back, of course. And you know how it went this last time."

"And now you're married again."

"Yes."

I frowned. "So you made a bad choice for yourself, and you would rather not have to make the choice again?"

"No. There's always a choice," she told me, not at all offended by my bluntness. "But if you want it simplified, I'll say this. Elak was a bad husband, and a bad father. Norath is a good man. He is an excellent husband and a delightful father."

"I see."

"I don't know if you do see," Nanaj said gently. "Marriage is an important part of village life. In a marriage, we rely on each other for companionship. For sustenance. For everything. Being married to Elak was not what marriage is supposed to be. Not at all. And I trust Gavril's judgement completely."

"I'm not asking about Gavril," I protested.

"Ah."

I busied myself with needlessly rocking her now-sleeping son.

"We've all heard that Taras has expressed an interest..." Nanaj trailed off as my face went red.

"All?"

"It's not a bad thing," she replied.

"Which part?" I forced a laugh.

"All of it," Nanaj said sincerely.

"Taras thinks I'm a part of some story." I couldn't keep the desperate edge out of my voice.

"He does?"

Something about the disinterest in her tone made me look up.

"Is that what *you* think?" I wanted to know. "Is that what everyone thinks?"

"Not everyone," Nanaj disagreed.

"What does that mean?"

"It means just what I said it means."

"I think it means something more," I persisted.

"Taras can believe what he likes," she told me. "Other people can believe what they like. In this, it only matters what Lanka and Duscna and Jereni think."

"Those two women who hate me?"

Nanaj laughed. "They don't hate you. They just don't want to make another mistake."

"Another one?"

She let out a sigh. "What do you know of the first woman Taras wanted to marry?"

"Just that she existed, and only because Gavril made sure I knew," I admitted. "Taras hasn't spoken of her himself."

"Taras and Gavril have never seen eye to eye, but their involvement with that woman was the end of any hope that they would get along. And it caused a rift between Jereni and Duscna and my mother, too."

She sat down at the table, and then motioned for me to join her.

"First, I must explain to you that we do not often speak of those who are gone," she said hesitantly. "To do so is considered bad luck."

"You don't have to tell me."

She smiled at me. "Sometimes there are things more important than superstition, and this is one of those things."

"Thank you," I replied, not bothering to hide my relief.

"The woman's name was Talia," Nanaj told me. "And she came from the other side of our land. From the village there."

"She was an Outsider? The ones who the Guard are fighting?"

My friend nodded, looking relieved that she wasn't going to have to explain that part of things.

"When Talia was a child, she was left on the edge of our village. A decoy. A trick, to draw out the Guard."

"That's awful."

"It gets much worse. Have you been told that the Outsiders mark themselves? Permanently?"

"No," I answered.

She shook her head. "It's so that we can't infiltrate them. They must think quite highly of themselves, to assume that we would try. They put the mark here."

Nanaj pinched the skin between her thumb and forefinger.

"They do it in a ceremony when the babies are just five days old. The mark is red on the girls, and black on the boys. It is a pattern that looks like this."

Nanaj pulled my good hand away from her son's back, and traced a four-pointed star. The baby shifted in my arms, and she took him from me. She kissed his tiny cheek and cradled him tightly against her body.

"When they left Talia, she was barely more than a baby herself, maybe five seasons at the most. The Outsiders wished to hide her origins. Or maybe they just wanted us to conclude that they had rejected her. So they decided to rid her of the identifying mark by cutting off her hand," Nanaj said. "Lanka's husband – mine and Taras's father – found her in the snow, shivering and near death. He knew that she was an Outsider, but he couldn't leave a child to die. When he attempted rescue, the Outsiders killed him before any of the Guard could stop them. We lost many men that day. But they were eventually triumphant. When the Guard brought Talia back to the village, Lanka took it upon herself to keep the girl. She raised her in our home."

"Oh."

The story chilled me.

"Talia was a pretty child, and clever, too. I would say she was manipulative, but that would imply that she had ill intentions. It would be more accurate to say that she didn't really know how to be any other way," Nanaj explained. "It was too easy to love with her. And Gavril did. She was my age, and she would follow him around. He was very indulgent, though she was several seasons younger than him. He was quite sweet with her. "

"Gavril?" I couldn't keep the surprise out my voice.

My friend laughed. "Yes, Gavril. From the second the Guard brought her home, he was as enchanted with her as she was with him. And as they got older, it was obvious to all that it was becoming something more"

"But they didn't get married?" I asked.

She shook her head. "For a long time, it did seem like it was going to happen that way. They spent a lot of time together, especially once Talia reached a marriageable age. And then Taras heard the legend for the first time. He became fixated on it."

"Taras believed that Talia was the woman in the story" I concluded.

"Yes," Nanaj agreed. "Many of the People did – including Jereni and Duscna. They backed up his claim to marry her, and were vocal in their belief that she was the girl."

"I see," I replied, feeling oddly relieved.

If the entire village had been wrong once, they could easily be wrong again, whether the two older woman wanted to be or not.

"Until then, Taras had more or less ignored her. I think he blamed her for our father's death, actually. But once he'd decided she was the one, he pursued her aggressively," Nanaj went on. "At first, Gavril disregarded his brother, as did Talia. But Taras is single-minded in his pursuits, and when it became obvious that Talia was becoming more and more interested, Gavril stepped away completely. He left the village for many months, and while he was gone, Taras requested permission to marry Talia. And Lanka approved."

"But she didn't think Talia was the woman in the story," I stated.

Nanaj nodded. "She was fine with Taras marrying her. She saw no reason for it not to happen. But she believed that Talia was ordinary. It put her in an awkward position. Because if Talia was not the legendary girl, then approving of her marriage to Taras meant that Taras, also, was ordinary."

"What happened?"

"Talia died before they could wed."

The look on Nanaj's face said that there was more to it than that, but I didn't pressure her.

"And when she died, Lanka was no longer on the spot. She was right – Talia was not the woman from the story. But Taras might still be the prophesied leader. Her death hit many hard, though none as hard as Taras. He couldn't make sense of it at all. He'd been so sure that Talia was the one. She fit the legend perfectly. Her hand. Her beauty. Her effect on all those around her."

"And yet he was mistaken."

"So it would seem."

"And now he thinks that it might be me."

"If he wants to lead the People, he must be careful not to be wrong again about something so important. The woman in the story is meant to change our course, to *reshape* the People."

Suddenly, Taras's careful kisses had new meaning. He had to be sure. He couldn't afford an error like the one he'd made with Talia. It would make him appear weak.

"You see?" Nanaj asked.

"Yes. I think that I do."

"Many believe that the story is utterly true. Most see it as absolute prophecy," my friend added.

"What do you think, Nanaj?" I wanted to know.

She considered my question carefully before she answered.

"I think that prophecy is meant to...unfold," she said slowly. "We don't need to force it to do so. That would defeat the purpose of it being prophecy. Do you agree?"

I nodded emphatically.

I had other questions, but Nanaj's son began to fuss, Andrik came running in, demanding food and attention, and I knew that it would have to wait.

Chapter Twelve

"Would you like to try something new?" Lanka asked.

"New how?"

"A new job."

Gavril stiffened at her words. His hand was raised to lift a piece of bread to his mouth, and for one second I thought that he was going to drop it. He hadn't spoken to me since our odd argument the previous afternoon.

"Like what?" I replied.

"Sewing?" she suggested.

I lifted my nearly-healed hand up questioningly.

"If you don't think you're strong enough..." Lanka trailed off and raised an eyebrow.

"I'll be fine," I replied, not really knowing if it was true, but knowing she'd be disappointed if I didn't rise to her obvious challenge. "So long as Gavril doesn't mind working without me."

He grunted. "Go where you're needed."

It was my turn to pause. I felt disappointed. I hadn't exactly expected him to jump in and say how much he appreciated my help, but it still hurt my feelings that he would dismiss me so quickly. Maybe he really *was* sorry he'd kissed me back.

Lanka grabbed her empty bowl and carried it over to the steaming pot of hot water where it would be washed out, leaving us alone for a moment.

"You don't want my help anymore?" I asked Gavril in a whisper.

"It seems like a bad idea," he replied coolly.

"You said you were sorry," I told him. "I think that's good enough."

"I am sorry," he said. "But I think it will be easier on me if I keep my distance."

"Easier on you?" I choked out. "What about what's easier for me?"

"That doesn't matter."

I tried to cover my hurt.

"I can start today," I told Lanka loudly.

She turned to us and raised an eyebrow again, but didn't argue.

"I'll take you there after breakfast," she said after the briefest of pauses.

"Perfect," I lied, and went back to eating

***

I hadn't lifted a needle since high school, and I was totally shocked to discover that I actually enjoyed sewing.

It was satisfying. At home if one of my shirts got a hole in it, I tossed it into the donation bin. But in the village, everything was sewn up, reused, and even resized if necessary.

I was given the task of repairing parkas. It was done with a large needle, and required surprisingly little manual dexterity. My hand did ache at the end of the first shift, but after a few days had gone by, I felt like it was actually making me stronger.

It was also reasonably solitary, which pleased me. Only two people were ever present in the sewing room – me, and the mute, elderly woman who had given me my bath on my first night in the village.

We worked in total silence, and that suited me just fine.

I was in the middle of reinforcing some well-used jackets one morning when a shadow suddenly blocked the light from the extra-wide oil lamp we used for good lighting.

"Hey!" I said in English.

"Hey to you," replied a gruff voice, also in English.

I looked up in surprise.

Gavril was smiling – a little nervously – down at me. "I've been listening to you talk to yourself. I thought I would give it a try."

"You did well," I told him.

He bowed. "Thank you."

I eyed him suspiciously. For Gavril, he was downright cheerful, and I didn't know what to make of it.

"What's the matter?" I asked.

Gavril laughed. "I have something to show you. If Satu is done with you, of course."

"Who's Satu?"

Gavril raised an eyebrow and gave a nod toward the older woman sitting beside me. She looked from me to him and then sighed.

"Take her," she said.

"You can talk?" I asked.

"If I have something to say."

Gavril laughed again, and reached down to help me up. He held my coat out for me, too, and I refrained from commenting until we were buttoned in between the two sets of tent flaps and out of Satu's earshot.

"No really," I said. "What's wrong?"

"Close your eyes," Gavril suggested.

"Seriously?"

"Seriously," he agreed. "I'll guide you."

With an exaggerated sigh, I lifted my mittens up to cover my face. He placed an arm around my waist and led me out into the cold. I tried my damnedest to *not* enjoy being pushed up beside him. I failed.

"Can I look?" I asked.

"Not yet."

We walked slowly, with Gavril murmuring a warning each time the path became uneven. His arm was still around me, and I wondered if people were watching us. My face warmed at what they might think.

"Almost there," Gavril said. "We're going to climb three steps, and then I'm going to help you sit."

He put both hands on my hips and guided me up, then down. Something soft and warm protected me from the snow-packed ground. I felt Gavril settle himself beside me.

"Lean back," he instructed.

I did, and my shoulders met with a hard surface.

"Okay," Gavril said. "Open your eyes."

I did, and I was surprised to be greeted by a reddish glow that bathed the village in its light. We were sitting on fur blankets, piled on top of an ice-covered roof. And they were warm. I pressed my hands against the blankets, wondering how they were holding the heat.

"Hot, crushed rocks," Gavril answered my unasked question.

I gazed around. The red light was becoming a blinding orange beacon, and it reflected off the snow, making the village look as though it had been set on fire. I could see that we weren't the only ones huddled on the low tops of the sunken-in dwellings.

"There," Gavril said, pointing in the direction that everyone else was already looking.

The sun peeked up from behind the mountains in the east. It had been so long since I'd seen it that the sight of it made my eyes well up.

"Amazing," I breathed.

"It won't last long," he warned.

He was right. After only a few minutes, the sun dipped back down, fading from orange to red to purplish grey, and it was perma-twilight once again. People climbed down off the roofs, and went back to their business.

"Thank you, Gavril," I said.

He placed his hand over top of mine.

"Would you like to go for a walk?" he asked politely.

"Sure," I agreed nervously.

I couldn't help but remember that it was very nearly the same question that Taras had asked me before telling me the story about the woman in the prophecy.

We climbed down, and Gavril led me away from the village and out into the hilly area where Andrik liked to collect rocks.

"You're not leading me to an execution, are you?" I teased with forced lightness.

Gavril frowned, and I knew that my joke had been lost in the translation.

With a grin, I made a slicing motion across my neck and added a gagging noise for extra effect.

Gavril laughed.

We continued walking, and he didn't let go of my hand. The air was crisp, but not too cold, and I felt like the few moments of sunshine had added brightness not just to the day, but to life in general.

We went past the hill where Taras and I had watched the Northern Lights and kept going.

Gavril didn't push the pace, and I actually managed to keep up without getting sweaty. We continued for quite some time, and when we finally did stop, it felt odd to be so still.

"Do you see that?" he wanted to know.

I peered through the greyness, and spied what he was referring to. He was looking down at the ground about five feet in front of us. It was a sheet of ice.

"Underneath it, there's water. And a yellow flower – dormant during the freezing time – waits for the thaw," Gavril told me. "When that happens, I will pick some for you."

And I wasn't able to hold it in any longer. "Why are you being so nice to me?"

"Are you happy here?" he replied evasively.

"I'm not *un*happy."

"Do you miss your family? Your friends? The food of your people?"

I swallowed. "I have no family. I miss my friend Sadie like crazy. And I would love a slice of pizza."

"Pizza?" Gavril tried the word out.

I smiled. "It's flat bread with sauce and something on top called cheese."

"Cheese?"

"Made from milk."

"Milk?"

"Stop that."

I tried to describe what I meant, using reindeer as a reference, and Gavril made a face.

"It sounds disgusting."

"It's delicious," I argued. "Don't be narrow-minded."

"Do you find the People to be narrow-minded quite often?" he asked.

I thought about it. It was an odd question and I didn't have an easy answer.

"Yes. And no. If one of the People crashed into my world as I did into yours, she would not be treated as a guest. She would be poked. And questioned. And probably sent away," I said. "But... The People do not explore, or look for what might be beyond their land. I'm not even sure that most of you consider that there is something else out there."

"I believe that there is," Gavril replied.

"Yes," I agreed. "You probably do. But it scares you, so you don't look for it."

"I wouldn't say that I fear the unknown," Gavril said. "But that doesn't mean I want to jump foolishly into it, either."

And maybe that was why, where so many of the People had accepted my presence as a matter of course, Gavril had been resistant. Maybe he viewed me as a threat to their way of life. And Lanka had warned me that he was traditional.

I looked at his face, trying to read it. He kept his emotions veiled.

"So," he said, "You might say that my people have open hearts, but limited scope. And the reverse is true of your people?"

"Yes, I might say exactly that."

"Do you have an open mind, like your people, Lindsay?" he asked.

"I like to think that I do," I replied.

"I would like to make you an offer," Gavril said softly. "And I believe that in order to accept it, you will also require an open heart, like us. Like me."

"All right."

A flurry of butterflies battered themselves against my stomach.

"Marry me."

"What?"

The suggestion floored me.

"I know that Taras is a good match," Gavril stated. "A warrior. A natural leader. He is reliable. Virtuous. A courageous man."

"Yes," I agreed. "From what I have seen, he is those things."

He frowned slightly.

Had he been expecting me to argue? To say that his brother lacked some of those characteristics?

"I don't believe that you wish to marry Taras," he said. "And I would like to give you an option."

The butterflies stopped abruptly, and irritation took their place. I did my best to keep it in check.

"And you see yourself as this option?" I asked tonelessly.

"I could be."

"I see."

Gavril nodded as if I had agreed with him. "Taras wants you for all the wrong reasons."

"Does he," I said flatly.

"There's more to the story that he told you on night he arrived from the hunt. He—"

I cut him off. "I know all about the legend."

"Then you know that my brother would do anything to further his claim. He would marry a reindeer if he thought it would fulfill this so-called prophecy."

"A reindeer." I bit the word off angrily, but Gavril didn't notice.

He laughed. "If Taras thought that it would help him achieve his goal of leading the People, there is nothing he wouldn't consider."

"So I'm the reindeer?" I asked.

"No. Not you." He frowned, and finally caught the look on my face.

I shook my head. "Are you that jealous of your brother?"

"Jealous?" Gavril sounded confused. "Jealous of what?"

"Of Taras leading the People!" I almost-yelled. "Do you think it should be *you*? I know that you're the son of... Somebody or other important. You made that abundantly clear when you chose Nanaj's husband for her."

"I do not—"

I didn't let him finish. "You don't get to pick a husband for me! I'm not of your people."

Gavril's eyes went cold. "And yet, you would still consider his proposal? To help him further his ambition."

"What ambition?" I demanded angrily. "You've already listed off his qualifications. It seems to me that he has nothing to do but sit back and enjoy his role."

"I don't know what you've been told," he said. "But Taras is not yet the leader of the People. Yes, he wants it.

But the role has not been claimed for generations for a good reason. It is not as simple as he sees it."

I watched his face as he spoke. I could see that he was telling the truth. Or at least believed it to be true.

"When my brother told you of the legend, he may have withheld an important detail," Gavril added.

"And what is that?"

"In order for Taras to claim the role of leader, he *must* marry the girl in the story, not the other way around. He won't be the leader and then marry her. He has to marry the girl in order to become our leader. That's what the prophecy says," he told me.

"And you don't want Taras to claim it?" I asked.

"Are you the girl in the legend?" he countered.

"No," I said.

"Taras thinks so. I don't. I'm not fond of prophecy in general. And I don't care if he leads or if he does not. All I care about is—" Gavril cut himself off. "Don't you see? If he marries you, and one of your *boats* comes to claim you, do you think my brother will let you go? He sees things only in terms of the good of the People. There is nothing he would not do on our behalf. He couldn't possibly release you."

"And you could? Release me?"

"I wouldn't try to hold you."

"So you would give me an option," I said quietly.

He nodded curtly. "It would save both you and my brother a lot of heartache."

And nothing else? No other reason? I wondered.

The rough feel of Gavril's mouth wasn't far from my mind. My lips burned now, just thinking of it. I could easily imagine his palms, working their way under my tunic, brushing the delicate skin on my stomach...

Gavril stood staring at me, and I thought I saw heat in his eyes.

Maybe I don't want to get married! I wanted to shout. *I left my last boyfriend because I didn't want to.*

But when I met his eyes, my mouth went dry.

"I would like something more than an option," I managed to whisper.

He stepped toward me, and I tipped my head up with embarrassing eagerness. He tossed his hood back, and leaned down. And then he stopped.

"I'm sorry," I said automatically. "I know you don't feel that way about me."

But something in the distance had caught his attention. I turned to follow his gaze, but couldn't see a thing.

He was listening intently. I strained to hear.

A horn. Somewhere near the village.

I looked back at Gavril, and I couldn't hold back a shiver. There was fear in his eyes.

"What is it?" I asked.

"Run!" he shouted.

Gavril darted across the tundra, and I struggled to keep up. He was surefooted and moved quickly. I stumbled and fell, breathing hard.

"Lindsay."

I stared up at him. "Sorry. I know you don't like me."

"No. That's not it. I—" he paused, and the pain in his eyes was palpable. "I'm sorry."

He reached down, lifted me up, and carried me until we could see the village clearly on the horizon. Then he put me down apologetically and sprinted the rest of the way.

***

"Hello!" I called out.

The pathways between the houses were empty.

I don't know what I had anticipated finding when I finally caught up, but a ghost town wasn't it.

"Gavril!" I shouted.

I made my way toward his house, feeling more panicked by the second. When an arm snaked out of nowhere and gripped my parka roughly, I screamed.

"Lin-zee!"

It was Nanaj.

"Get inside. Quickly," she hissed.

She darted back into her house, and I had no choice but to follow.

"What's going on?" I asked.

In her house, nothing seemed out of place. My friend's kids were lying on a blanket. Andrik was shaking a bone rattle, and the baby was cooing contentedly.

"Everyone has been ordered indoors," Nanaj told me. "Lanka and the others are in an emergency meeting."

"What? Why? Was the village attacked?"

She shook her head. "Worse. The Guard has fallen."

Shock immobilized me.

"How do you know?"

"A short time ago, two men came into the camp. One was Artyom, the young man selected to cook for the Guard. The second was one of *them*. An Outsider. He held a knife to Artyom's throat and demanded to speak to Gavril. When he couldn't be located, the Outsider demanded that Artyom tell us what had happened. Artyom was terrified, but the Outsider told him that if he told us exactly what had happened, his life would be spared. Lin-zee, I have never seen someone so frightened." Nanaj began to cry as she spoke. "Artyom said that the Outsiders had overwhelmed the Guard. That they had come in from behind and burned down their camp. He told us that all were captured or dead, and that they were willing to make a trade."

"A trade?"

"If Gavril…If he sacrifices himself, they will let the others go."

"If Gavril... Why, Nanaj?" I asked.

"It's not my place to tell you."

"Please."

"Lin-zee..."

"Please." I couldn't keep the desperation out of my voice.

"Revenge."

"I don't understand."

"You must not share this with anyone. And you must not tell Gavril that you know," she cautioned.

"All right."

"It's about Talia, the woman Taras was meant to marry."

"Tell me."

"Shortly after Taras and Talia became engaged, he left for Guard duty. As I told you before, Gavril had left the village before their engagement was announced, and he hadn't yet returned. Talia decided that my brothers should reconcile before the wedding. She went out on her own, convinced that she would find Gavril. I don't know what made her do it, or why she chose that exact time to speak with Gavril. Maybe she thought it would be better if they were truly alone. But not long after she left, Talia encountered a party of Outsiders who had become separated from the main unit. They were lost, and unusually close to our village. This group of men...They found Talia. They beat her and they raped her, and they killed her slowly," Nanaj said bitterly. "With the Guard still gone, and a sudden storm coming on, Gavril decided to return to the village. He was made aware of her absence immediately, and he set out to retrieve her in spite of the snow. He found her broken and frozen body. And then he found the men who had done it. They were huddled in a cave, trying to weather the storm."

"Oh," I said softly, feeling a large lump form in my throat.

"He felt responsible," she explained. "Because she was searching for him. He didn't leave any of the Outsiders alive, Lin-zee."

"Oh."

"He killed them, strung them to his sled, and dragged them to the edge of our territory, where the Guard had just driven back the rest of the Outsiders. And then he kept going, right into their land. He marched into their village and dropped what was left of the bodies in the middle of the main path. And among those he killed was the only son of their leader."

"Why didn't they kill him in return?"

Nanaj shrugged. "Their own men weren't back yet from the battle with ours. It was just the women and children. Gavril explained to them in blunt terms what had happened, and then came home. No one tried to stop him."

I stared at her, rendered silent by the story.

"Did he tell you all of this?" I asked.

"No," she replied. "Some if came from Lanka, some from the men on the Guard. And some from a witness in the Outsiders' village."

Norath came through the door at that moment.

"You're just in time. Take off your gloves," she told him. "Show her."

He frowned slightly but obeyed her request. He pulled them off and lifted his hands up so that I could see the large, faded black star in between his thumb and his forefinger.

"Norath's father fled the Outsiders village when my husband was just a child," Nanaj explained. "He left because when his wife told him what had been done to Talia, he couldn't bear it. She was his daughter, you see. Norath's sister. They had nowhere to run but here."

I was overwhelmed.

"You look ill," my friend said to me.

"I feel it."

Norath put his gloves back on and smiled apologetically.

"My love," he said. "Gavril and I are going."

"Going where?" But I already knew the answer.

"If there's a chance to save even one life, Gavril will take it." Norath directed the answer toward me. "Especially if that life is Taras's."

"Yes," Nanaj agreed softly. "I wish you didn't have to."

"I have to go, because there's no one else," Norath added.

I said nothing, because I felt like I'd had the wind knocked out of me.

***

Because of the snow, I hadn't seen the flurry of activity that had surrounded the departure of Taras and the Guard, but as I watched Gavril and Norath prepare to leave, I imagined it times sixty.

There seemed to be an impossible amount of things to do, and no time to do them.

Spears had to be readied, food – mostly a granola mix and dried meat – had to be packed. Layers of clothing and sleep gear for travelling needed to be bundled.

Within an hour, Gavril and Norath were standing at the edge of the village, looking large and dangerous.

The entire population had come out to see them off, and the solemnity of the occasion was apparent in their faces.

Gavril met and held my gaze for just one moment, and then they set off at a slow jog.

***

By the time they were no longer visible, I felt very odd. Dizzy, and a little disoriented. My legs were shaking, too. I tried to walk, but had to stop.

"Lanka!" I called.

I wasn't sure how close I was to Gavril's dwelling, or even if I'd still be staying there. As I blinked, my vision became blurred. The tops of the houses all looked the same.

"Lanka!" I called again, more weakly than before.

Where did she go? I wondered.

I stumbled forward, and I almost fell. I looked down at my feet, wondering why they weren't working properly. I raised my eyes, and I thought I saw Lanka in the distance, standing in front of a doorway.

I walked toward her, bringing one foot forcibly in front of the other. I felt as though I wasn't making any progress, and I gasped with the effort. At last, an arm encircled my waist.

"Lin-zee, it will be okay." It was Lanka's voice.

I drew in a breath, and it was then that I realized I was sobbing.

***

The days passed in a seemingly wool-wrapped haze.

The sun came up a little more each day, but I hardly noticed.

I did the jobs Lanka assigned me with speed and accuracy, but with no passion. She kept trying, and I kept smiling apologetically.

I felt the same as I had right after I learned my mother died, and when I realized that, I realized why.

I was grieving.

***

"Lin-zee."

I rolled over at the sound of my name being whispered in the dark

"Lin-zee."

I rolled over again, then sat up slowly.

Andrik was bouncing on my bed, looking hopeful.

"What is it?" I asked.

"They're coming back."

"Gavril and Norath?"

Andrik shook his head. "The Guard."

"What do you mean?"

"They're heading into the village now."

I scrambled out of bed with a thick lump in my throat and followed the little boy out into the street without bothering to put on my coat. I knew that if they were coming back, Gavril must've caught up with them.

What did that mean for him?

This time, as the men marched back into the village, no one cheered. Instead, a horrified stillness overcame the People as their hunters trudged down the main path. I found that I was holding my breath as they approached the area where I stood.

I took in their appearance, and fear overwhelmed me.

Their parkas were dirty, and some of the staining looked like blood. Many were limping, and as they got closer, I realized that several were being carried on handmade stretchers.

Taras led the way, and though he held his head high, there was something in his demeanor that screamed defeat.

When the thick of them had reached the centre of the village, they stopped as one, and knelt down.

Taras remained standing, and he immediately commanded the attention of everyone within earshot.

"Family," he said in a voice that carried. "The Guard has not failed."

There was a whisper of relief from the crowd, but it was followed quickly by a whisper of confusion.

Taras nodded. "We drove them back, though imperfectly. One has given his life. Two more will likely perish before nightfall. And eight are grievously wounded. But the children of our village are safe."

My heart ached for the loss of life. But Taras's words had a victorious tone.

Why then, was his expression so sorrowful? I wondered. *Gavril. Where was Gavril? One life...*

All of the blood rushed to my head.

"Taras!" I tried to call out.

It came out no louder than a whisper.

I moved toward him, but as I did, the rest of the men stood, and I lost sight of him in the crowd. As they made their way to their wives and home, I pushed through them, seeking his hawk-like face. At last, the throng of weary men began to thin out, and I realized why I was having such a hard time finding him.

Taras was now bent down on one knee, hugging Andrik tightly. When he saw me approaching, he released his nephew and whispered for him to go. Then he put his arms out, and I let him pull me into his lap and embrace me. He gripped me loosely, and kissed each of my cheeks lightly.

"Such a relief to see you," he murmured into my hair.

"I'm glad you are safe," I replied. "Was it bad?"

It wasn't the question I wanted to ask, but it felt impolite to skip straight to asking about his brother.

"This was a trying mission."

"But you were successful."

"They were more cohesive this season," he mused. "They're always brutal. And forceful. But rarely so organized."

"Do you often lose men?" I asked with a thickness in my voice that I couldn't hide.

"Not every time."

Taras's features darkened, and regret touched his eyes.

"And your brother?" I asked softly, forcing myself to say his name. "Gavril?"

Taras shook his head, and I knew the source of the pained look on his face. I felt my own features fall, and my breath stuck in my throat. In seconds, my cheeks were wet with tears.

I rested my head on Taras's shoulder for just a moment, wondering if I could live like this for the rest of my life. If I could imagine never going home. If I could be the wife of this man, who led a village like this one.

Could I do it?

Could I take the risk?

Could I live with the idea that at any moment, on any given day, I might lose my husband as I had lost Gavril?

Why consider it now? demanded a small voice in my head. *Because Gavril is gone? Because now there is no chance that you and he—*

I cut the voice off.

I needed to fill the void.

"Taras," I whispered.

"Yes?"

The words stuck in my throat.

"Do you hesitate, even now?" Taras asked, as if he could he hear my thoughts.

He tipped my chin up toward him and examined my expression. I felt like a child, staring up at his serious face.

I wanted to ask him about his brother again, but I remembered what Nanaj had told me about speaking of the dead.

"No," I said at last. "I'm ready."

Taras's face lit up. "We'll do it now."

"Now?"

"I know that Lanka wishes us to wait. But the People need a celebration," he told me quietly. "To take their minds off this tragedy."

I remembered what Gavril had said about Taras always putting the good of the People ahead of his own desires. While it didn't slip by me that at the moment the two needs overlapped conveniently, Taras's words seemed too true to refute.

Chapter Thirteen

"Isn't it funny?" I asked. "It takes less time to get ready for a wedding than it does to go off to kill a man?"

I didn't even realize that I had spoken in English until Nanaj shook her head in confusion.

"Sorry," I apologized. "I guess I'm nervous."

I was more than nervous. I was terrified, and I'd been brushing off the pervasive feeling that I was making a mistake. But I wasn't going to back out. I wasn't going to revert to my second guessing ways.

And at least if I married Taras, I'd be serving a greater purpose for the Village.

My friend smiled at me, and adjusted my dress. It was made of the same woven material as the tunics, but it was dyed a vicious shade of red, and it touched my knees. The neckline scooped low, and was embroidered with brown flowers. Satu had prepared the pieces, and when they were ready, she'd sewn the dress right onto my body.

If I have to pee, I'm screwed, I thought.

Nanaj smiled at me. "Don't worry. It will be over quickly. Both of my weddings were."

I laughed, but stopped myself abruptly when it almost turned into a sob.

"It's selfish of me to do this while Norath is injured," I said.

"I don't believe that it's selfish. He wouldn't think so either," she argued.

I disagreed, but I didn't say it. My friend's husband was one of the ones whom Taras described as grievously injured. He had been carried in on a stretcher, and had remained in a semi-conscious state since their arrival. Nanaj seemed sure that he would wake up, and kept dismissing my concerns.

Taras had made the announcement within minutes of my acceptance, and I hadn't been given a moment to think since then.

I had received a spa treatment, complete with mud wrap and a rub that removed the hair from everywhere but my head. I'd spent what felt like hours memorizing the formal vows – the words were the most important part of the ceremony, apparently. And I hadn't been allowed to speak to Taras even once.

The two oldest women in the village – Duscna and Jereni, as it turned out – were in charge of the whole affair, and they dealt with me in tight-lipped silence. They hadn't released me to Nanaj until they were sure that I was up to their grimly high standards. And even then, they had admonished my friend to stick carefully to tradition.

"If she is to be his wife," Jereni had said, "Then we had best do this right."

Duscna had just snorted.

I sighed as Nanaj made an adjustment to my hair. It was coiled into eight skinny braids.

"I might throw up," I admitted to my friend.

"Don't do it on Taras's feet," she advised.

"I can't promise that."

I swallowed nervously, glad that I'd been forced to fast. I hadn't eaten since supper the previous evening.

Had it really only been fifteen or so hours since I had agreed to this wedding?

"Are you sure that this is the right decision?" Nanaj asked suddenly.

She was scrutinizing my face.

I nodded.

"What've I got to lose?" I answered lightly.

***

Taras stood just inside the makeshift tent that had been hastily erected in the centre of the village. He was flanked by two of the Guard. When he glanced at me, his mouth opened just a little in what I hoped was admiration. The two Guardsmen nodded at me and then shuffled a little so that Taras was standing slightly in front of them.

I stepped nervously into the tent, ignoring the stares of the People as they caught sight of me. Nanaj had explained that weddings were usually limited to immediate family and elders, but that Taras had insisted on inviting everyone in the village. It was the one tradition that Duscna and Jereni had agreed to overlook.

Taras smiled at me confidently. It was impossible to not feel self-conscious with almost two hundred sets of eyes trained on me as I made my way toward my husband-to-be.

His new suede pants hugged his hips in a flattering way, and his off-white tunic exposed a large portion of his muscular chest.

I breathed carefully through my nose, and gripped Lanka's hand tightly when she came to lead me to the front of the tent.

"You remember the words?" she whispered.

I nodded. My throat was too dry to speak.

Lanka put a hand on my elbow and began guiding me toward Taras. I felt the eyes of the People following us as we went. When I reached Taras's side, he took my good hand and squeezed it gently.

"Lovely," he said quietly.

I saw Duscna's eyes tighten, and I tensed. Taras wasn't supposed to speak to me until I started reciting the vows. I tried to smile at her, and I saw her face darken. But she wasn't looking at me. She was staring at the doorway. I turned my head automatically, and caught sight of what was holding the older woman's gaze.

Nanaj was standing at the entryway with her husband propped on her arm. He looked weak, and tired, and his face hung even more slack than usual.

"Gavril," my friend said softly.

I froze.

Her voice had carried through the tent. And she was clearly waiting for me to answer her.

"I thought that it was inappropriate to speak of the dead," I replied stiffly.

"You must speak to Norath," she told me.

"This isn't the time," Jereni said while Duscna nodded her agreement.

"Leave us," Taras suggested suddenly. "Now. All of you. You, too, Norath."

There was a moment of shocked silence, and then the People shuffled noisily out of the tent.

It felt like an eternity, waiting for everyone to go. When we were finally alone, I said his brother's name questioningly.

"Gavril?"

Taras reached his arms out and grasped my shoulders.

"My brother is a good man," he said in a quiet and sincere voice. "In spite of our differences, I'm fond of him. This will be a great loss for the tribe..."

Taras continued speaking, but I couldn't hear him any longer. My entire body was prickling in a painful way. I thought that I must have been vibrating with the sensation. Taras didn't notice.

"You said *is*," I interrupted.

"What?"

"You said that Gavril *is* a good man."

"Yes."

"He's not dead?"

"He was alive when I left him, but, Lin-zee..."

I heard myself hiss. "You left him?"

"They were on him before we could react. It happened more quickly than I would ever have thought possible," Taras told me calmly. "We weren't even expecting him. Do you know *why* he and Norath came?"

To save you.

But I couldn't talk. I was too angry.

"You know, their retreat began nearly the second they had him," Taras sounded just the slightest bit puzzled. "It was almost as though their goal was to capture him, and no one else."

I finally found my voice. "Did no one tell you? Not even Lanka?"

"I've been tending to the Guard and the details of the wedding." He shook his head.

Why had no one told him that Gavril had gone to save him? Had it just seemed so obvious that Taras ought to have figured it out on his own?

"Why did you leave him?" I demanded.

"They outnumbered us, two to one. This is usually true, but as I said, they were organized. They had weapons. We were unprepared for such an onslaught. Then they began the retreat. Many men would have died if we had pursued them, Lin-zee."

"But he's your brother."

Taras shrugged. "He would have done the same, had the positions been reversed."

I almost slapped him. There was no doubt in my mind that Gavril would have done anything, even sacrificed his own life, to save to Taras. In fact, he'd been more than willing to do it.

"Go back," I said. "Please go back."

"The Outsiders don't leave many prisoners alive. Only children and those who will join them. Gavril falls into neither category." Taras's voice was even and accepting.

"No," I said, jumping up.

Had I been ready to marry this man, just moments earlier?

He remained standing in front of me, and I stared up at him. I saw resignation, and nothing else. Maybe he'd assumed that I would take the news of Gavril's capture in the same matter-of-fact way that he had.

And something clicked. He did remind me of Ben, after all. Perfect by many people's standards. But not for me.

"I have to go," I told Taras.

"Where?"

But I was already fleeing, disregarding the cold as it wafted up my legs. I ran through the village, ignoring the looks I was getting.

Let them make whatever assumptions they want, I thought.

I headed straight for Gavril's house, and I was already forming a loose plan in my mind.

***

As I packed, I longed for Nanaj's company, but I knew that every second I wasted was a second that Taras could alert the village.

Alert them to what? The fact that I was leaving him at the altar? They'd probably want to run me out of town themselves when they found out.

I pushed the thoughts aside and dug guiltily through Gavril's room, searching for the items I knew I would need. Something to make fire. Something to sleep in. Extra clothes, just in case.

An unwilling image came to mind.

It was of Gavril, bound and gagged.

What if they've already killed him? demanded a small voice in my head.

I snarled at the voice angrily, and placed a few more items on the bed, then grabbed a little clay jar. It was full of a flammable, oil-based jelly. I would be easier to light than the tinder and flint that the People usually used to start a fire. I reached up to the shelf again, and something caught my eye.

It was shiny, and purple, and totally familiar. My shirt. The one I'd been wearing on the plane. I pulled it out slowly, and I as I did, it caught on something tucked in behind, knocking it to the ground.

I picked it up incredulously. It was a canvas backpack, printed with grey and blue stripes. I shook it and then emptied it. It was full of items that Gavril must have salvaged from the wreck.

Some of it was useless. There was a piece of charred seat belt, and a rusty metal screw. There was a crushed tube of lipstick, and a package of Lifesavers candy. There was a narrow piece of wood that didn't make any sense to me until I shook it. It was a retractable walking stick. And there were a few items that I quickly added to my pile. A compass. A dented metal water bottle. A bottle of pills. A thick, unbroken mirror.

And there was one thing in the bag that made my hands shake.

It was a gun.

I didn't know what kind, and I wasn't even sure how to fire it.

But I did know that all it would take was one shot to scare the pants off whoever was holding Gavril captive.

I gathered up all my things and began tucking them carefully into one of Gavril's wide packs. I put everything in except the seat belt and the purple blouse.

I added some flat bread, because I thought it might keep for a day or two, and some dried fish because I knew it would be good for as long as I was gone. I found a big linen pouch, full of granola, and carefully laid it between the bread and the fish. I folded up one of Gavril's tunics and used it to keep everything else in place.

"You'll need a bed," said a small voice from behind me.

"Hi, Andrik," I replied with a sigh.

"You're not going to marry Taras?"

"I'm afraid not."

"But you're going to save Gavril?"

"Who told you?" I asked.

"I just guessed," he said with a shrug.

"That's my plan," I admitted.

"Let me help you."

My little friend dug out a bedroll and explained to me how I needed to unroll it properly, then put the stiffened leather inside my fur sleeping bag. He rolled them up together and tied them firmly with a piece of leather cord.

"You should take some rope, too, just in case."

Andrik found two kinds – leather and linen – and handed them to me. I put them both in my bag.

"Do you remember how to build a shelter on the side of a hill?" he asked.

"I think so," I lied.

He sighed. "Find a hill about the same size as your body, and carve a space big enough for you to lie down in. If it's facing the wind, put up a leather sheet. Do you have a tent?"

"Not yet," I told him.

He disappeared for a few moments, then reappeared with a folded piece of leather.

"It's stronger than it looks," he said. "Do you want me to show you how to use it?"

"Is it hard?"

He grinned. "Not for me."

"Show me," I suggested.

He unfolded the leather, and I saw that the edges were reinforced with something very stiff, and that the corners were weighted on the inside with rocks. There were two foot-long pieces of wood, bound with leather, and curved into a bow-like shape. Andrik spread it all out, explaining how I needed to bury the rocks in the snow to keep it from blowing away, and how to plant the wood pieces on either side of the tent to keep it from collapsing. When it was set up in Gavril's living room, it barely looked big enough.

"So I just crawl inside?" I asked.

"It won't keep you very warm on its own," he warned as he nodded. "But it will keep you dry, and if it's windy, it will help."

"Andrik, you're smart," I said in English.

He smiled. "I know."

I put on my layers – two tunics, fur-lined pants, and my parka – then slipped into my boots and mittens. Andrik gave me another bag of food, and I stuck it into my pocket. Then I slid my pack onto my back, where it hung awkwardly to one side. My little friend laughed, and told me to take it off.

He laid the bag on the floor and attached the bedroll and sleeping bag to it with a wide piece of leather.

"When you're doing it yourself, tie them together first, and then slip them over your head," he said. "And you can put the tent in between so they don't move when you're walking."

"The things you can learn when you're not playing video games," I murmured in English.

"Put it over your head," Andrik instructed.

I picked up the whole thing, and slid my arms and head through the leather straps. It settled, not quite comfortably, into place and I smiled at Andrik.

I can do this, I thought.

And then I said it out loud, to make it real. "I can do this."

"I think so," Andrik agreed.

I was starting to sweat already. I grabbed my little friend and gave him a hug.

"Thank you."

He wriggled away.

"Don't travel in the dark, okay?" he suggested in a small voice.

"I won't," I promised. "You can count on it."

***

I walked straight through the village, pretending not to notice the odd looks I got as I went.

It was easy, at first, to follow the path left by the returning Guard. It hadn't snowed since they'd come back, and they hadn't been trying to hide their tracks.

Their path widened and narrowed as the frozen terrain allowed, and rarely seemed to waver away from straight west. The footprints sometimes went directly over crops of rock that I couldn't navigate, and each time that happened, I would skirt around the path, panicking that I wouldn't be able to find my way back to the trail.

I looked for signs of Gavril and Norath, but anything they might have left behind had been destroyed by the Guard.

My legs began to ache, and I could feel sweat dripping on the inside of my boots.

I kept going because I thought they would have.

I got hungry, and I ate from the bag Andrik had given me without stopping.

I tried to keep a steady pace, but it was difficult. Unpredictable rocks, and my own lack of experience slowed me down. I tossed my hood off, knowing that I'd get a sunburn, but I was too warm to care. My pack was weighing down on me, and my shoulders and arms were starting to protest.

Hiking through the tundra is harder than one of Sadie's stupid step classes, I thought, and then stumbled.

I hadn't thought of her in what seemed like a very long time.

She was always on a health kick of some time, and forever signing up for lunch time exercise classes. Zumba. Spinning. Pilates.

I usually ate a burger instead.

My stomach growled, and I glanced up at the sun, trying to figure out how long I'd been travelling.

"Long enough for the cubed bread and berries to have burned off," I muttered out loud.

I stopped guiltily. I needed a break.

I glanced up at the sun again. It looked like it might be going down, but I was terrible at judging the time. I wasn't even sure how much daylight we'd been getting. Not more than a few hours, I thought, and I'd been travelling since just after dawn.

Which is about when you should've been marrying Taras. The thought came involuntarily, and I pushed it aside.

I yanked my pack off and sat down on a large, lichen-covered rock.

Pull it together, I commanded myself.

I dug out a piece of dried fish and devoured it. I wanted another piece, but I just took a big gulp of water from my salvaged water bottle instead. When I was done drinking, I repacked the bottle with snow and put it away. Then I closed my eyes and let myself drift, just for a minute.

The air was cold, but it smelled different that it had near the village. It was earthier. I inhaled deeply, and then opened my eyes.

The sun really was going down. It seemed lower than it had been just minutes earlier. I squinted at it, realizing that the actual horizon looked different, too. I could see an indistinct tree line. Actually, it was more of a miniscule shrub line, but it was more foliage than I'd seen in the whole time I'd been there.

I jumped to my feet, ignoring the groaning protest my body made at the sudden movement. I shrugged back into my gear, and began walking again, feeling determined.

My legs disagreed with the decision, and after maybe thirty minutes, they threatened to give out from under me.

"Dammit," I muttered.

The shrub line was still very far off – probably several days' worth of travel – and the sun was going to be completely down very soon. I could feel a bit of wind, too, and when I looked up, I could see a few heavy clouds in the distance. I took a few more steps, then I gave up.

You are not *giving up,* I told myself. *You're just being practical.*

I needed the light to set up camp, and I wasn't even sure if I'd be able to get a proper fire started. And if it started to snow...

I shivered in response, automatically flexing my bad hand. I wasn't ready to go through that again.

I glanced around, searching for a good space to set up my tent. A tallish mound of snow-covered rock caught my eye, and I said a silent thank you to Andrik for his advice. I made my way toward it, and I felt momentarily elated when I reached the little hill. It was bigger than I had thought, and it had a wide dip at its base. It was the perfect place to set up.

I unfolded the tent, trying to follow my little friend's guidelines. When I was done, it looked lopsided, but serviceable. I unrolled my bedding and tucked it inside. I sat back and survey my handiwork. It wasn't perfect, but it would do.

A gust of wind cut through the air, and I was pleased to see that it didn't quite reach the tent.

After a quick consideration, and a glance at the darkening sky, I decided not to bother with a fire. I was tired, and eager to try out my accomplishment.

"Here goes," I said.

I pushed my pack into the tent, and crawled in after it. I squeezed myself into my fur-lined sleeping bag, and when I was properly tucked in, the flap at my feet swung shut. It was surprisingly warm, completely dark, and eerily silent. The only thing I could hear was the sound of my own breathing.

I closed my eyes, and in seconds, I was asleep.

***

When I woke up, my whole body was stiff. I stretched my arms out and bumped them against the interior of the leather tent. I met with heavy resistance from the outside and I panicked for just second before the reasonable part of my brain asserted that it must be snow.

I kicked out of my sleeping bag and pushed the flap open with my feet. Crisp air whipped into the tent, and as I wriggled out, I groaned. The sun was already visible on the horizon. I'd slept for too long, and I'd lost precious travel time.

Several inches of fresh snow covered my campsite, and my tent was almost invisible.

"Ugh," I said.

My stomach grumbled irritably, too, and I decided to eat before I packed up.

As I reached down to grab my pack out of the tent, the wind shifted, sending a cloud of powdery snow into my face.

I swore loudly, then froze as I caught the scent of roasting meat. I smelled it for just a second, before it was gone.

I strained my senses. I couldn't smell it anymore. But then I thought I heard something. It sounded like voices, very far away. Then that was gone, too.

I stood up, looking for signs of people or smoke. I trained my gaze in the direction of the path I'd been following the day before. The snow had mostly obscured it. I couldn't see any signs of life.

I sighed, yanked a piece of bread out of my bag, and settled on the edge of my bedroll to eat it. I took one bite, then smelled the meat again.

I groaned and wondered if I was experiencing some kind of nasal hallucination.

But I heard the voices again, too, and I stopped chewing.

I stood up for a second time, more slowly, and looked carefully in the other direction, over the top of my little hill. I sat down again very quickly.

A group of fur-clad men was standing around a largish fire about a hundred yards away. Each time the wind changed direction, I could smell their food and hear their voices. I stared at them for a few moments before my good sense took over and remembered that if I could see them, they could see me.

I crouched warily beside my tent. My heart was hammering in my chest. I knew they hadn't spotted me, or they would've already come running.

I turned around carefully, pressing myself against the angled hill, and slid up so that I could just see over the top. I slid my hood off, grateful for the first time since my arrival that my hair was so blonde. At least it would blend in with the snowy background.

The men were engrossed in their meal, and even from where I sat, I could make out a surprising amount of detail. I counted nine men, all bearded, and all big. Their parkas and boots looked muddy, and I wondered how long they'd been travelling. To a man, they appeared short-tempered.

One of them flung his arms up angrily, and I watched as another man shoved him in reply. They all tensed up, and I waited for a brawl to start. But a tenth man, shorter than the rest, popped up suddenly from the ground, and the rest of them went still.

The shorter man began pointing emphatically at the ground, and I wished that I could see what he was so interested in. Finally, one of the men made a surrendering motion and stalked over to the other side of the fire.

He reached down then jerked upright again, straining visibly.

I gasped.

"Gavril," I whispered.

It was him. I was sure of it.

His arms were limp, and I couldn't see his lower body. His head lolled to one side, and he looked as though he was unconscious. The man who held him up shook him, not lightly. And then Gavril's arm shot out, striking his captor forcefully in the gut. The man dropped him, and when he hit the ground, I couldn't see him anymore. But I had no problem making out the kicking motions as the man who'd let him go doled out his punishment. He drew his foot back, and I counted seven kicks. It took all of my willpower to hold in my screams. I slid back down to my tent, breathing deeply through my nose.

I needed a new plan.

The men hadn't set up a camp of any kind, but they also didn't look like they were preparing to leave.

I didn't know how much sun I had left, but it didn't really matter anyway. I'd found my target. And as long as they were positioned where they were, I couldn't make a move. The only thing keeping me from detection was my location.

I had no choice but to sit tight, count the minutes, and pray that none of Gavril's captors decided to come my way.

Chapter Fourteen

It was probably the longest few hours of my life. I'd never sat so long in one spot without something to occupy my hands or my mind.

I ate sporadically, and fell asleep twice, jerking awake both times when a gust of wind cut into my hood.

I debated about what to do with the tent. I didn't want to leave it, but I was afraid that taking it down was going to attract attention. Eventually, I decided not to risk it.

Finally, the sun started to dip down below the horizon, and I knew that I was going to have to move soon. My legs were nearly numb, and stretching in my sitting position wasn't helping anymore. I pulled myself up into a crouch. My legs instantly started to tingle, and I couldn't decide if the renewed blood flow was a good feeling or a bad one. I leaned against the hill and glanced over the ridge.

The men were still in exactly the same spot as they had been the other times I'd checked, and I wondered once again what they were waiting for. Most of them were sitting around the fire now, instead of standing. I couldn't see Gavril, but I knew that he was there somewhere.

I sat back down, and waited some more.

As dusk began to set in, I finally heard movement from their camp.

I risked another look.

They were packing up and dumping snow onto the fire.

Crap, I thought. *No wonder they haven't moved all day.*

They were going to travel at night to ensure that they weren't exposed.

Crap, I thought again as I watched them.

I was going to have to break my promise to Andrik.

The only advantage would be that I might have a better chance of sneaking up on them.

If you can keep up with them, I added mentally.

There were a few shouts from the men, and then they started to move. I watched them go, trying to take an inventory of their resources. The two leading the group carried spears casually on their shoulders. Four men pulled a small sled apiece, and two more men pulled a larger one between them. A final duo followed behind. One of them gripped a wood club, and the other appeared unarmed.

I waited until they were a good distance away before I started my pursuit.

I paused at their campfire site, feeling sick as I looked at the spot where Gavril had been kicked. I sat there for just a moment, contemplating my options. And then I was struck by sudden inspiration.

I pulled a small leather sack out of my big bag and filled it with ashes. It was an imperfect idea, but it was all I had.

I jumped up again, straining to see the men in the increasing darkness. I lagged behind because I worried that I was following too closely, but pretty soon I was sweating as I tried to keep up. They paid no attention to their surroundings, and didn't bother to look behind themselves at all.

They were fast, almost aggressive in their travel. I trudged along behind them, wincing each time one of the sleds hit a bump. I'd concluded that Gavril must be strapped to one of them.

They switched position occasionally, but seemed tireless. I was already exhausted, and we'd only been moving for a few hours or so.

Then suddenly they stopped.

I dove to the ground and huddled there, praying that they wouldn't look in my direction. But they were all staring at the sky.

I looked up, too.

Dark clouds were rolling in overhead, and I knew instantly why the men were so anxious.

A storm.

The men began to argue, and the short one stepped in again, issuing commands and pointing emphatically at the clouds. The others pulled out long sheets of leather, and I realized that they were going to put up tents.

I realized, also, that I was going to have to act quickly.

I watched them as they erected three tents, then built another large fire. They dragged the larger sled into the smallest tent, and when they pulled it out again, it was almost flat. I knew that they had unloaded Gavril inside.

The short man continued to give orders, and just as the snow started, they settled into their positions. Two men guarded Gavril's tent, two went into the larger one, and the rest gathered around the fire.

"Now or never," I murmured to myself.

I dropped my pack onto the ground and took my parka off. I removed both of my shirts, shoved one into the bag, and put the other aside. I shivered. It was cold, and getting colder. I moved as quickly as I could.

I dug out the ash-filled leather sack, and I was happy to see that none of it had spilled. I tugged on the strings, and it opened with an almost inaudible sigh.

PFFT.

I sniffed. There was nothing to be done about the sooty smell, but the ashes would serve their purpose. Taking a deep breath, I dumped them over my head, being careful not to inhale as they settled on my body. I rubbed the ashes into my hair, along my arms, and onto my face, then put my shirt back on.

I grabbed the mirror of my bag and squinted at myself. My hair was sticking up every which way and looked almost black. My face looked dirty, but it was impossible to tell the colour of my skin. I just had to hope that the men weren't going to be looking too closely at my eyes.

I put my bag on my back, tucked my sleeping bag around my stomach, and then finally put my parka on over top.

I took a deep breath, and walked straight toward the group of men who held Gavril captive.

***

The first to spot me was one of the men guarding Gavril's tent. His eyes widened, and he shook his head like he couldn't believe what he was seeing. I kept going, and at first he said nothing. But when I got a little too close, he shouted, right at me.

His language was accented, but otherwise identical to that of the People.

"Woman!" he shouted. "Woman!"

I wasn't sure if it was a greeting or a warning, and it didn't matter. I forced myself to ignore him, to pretend that I couldn't hear him. I continued to amble along, stumbling at what I hoped were irregular intervals. It wasn't much of a stretch – the terrain was uneven, and because I was looking everywhere but down, I tripped often.

I was almost to the very edge of the camp, still looking straight ahead, and still moving ever so slowly. I hoped that they couldn't tell I was approaching on purpose. As I meandered along the area near the fire, all of the men began to watch me. At first, they were wary, but as my random gait and non-threatening manner because apparent, they relaxed. Two of them actually laughed out loud at my progress, and after just a few moments, they began to call out to me.

"Careful!"

"Don't fall on that pretty face!"

"Is it a pretty face? I can't tell."

I almost laughed at the last comment, but I stifled it quickly.

Finally, when I was close enough to make out the details of their faces in the firelight, I collapsed dramatically on the ground. At first my fall was greeted by silence, then there was a flurry of movement, and I got the feeling that several of the men had moved to crouch over me. I kept very still, breathing unevenly. I didn't have to try very hard to feign the raggedness of my inhales and exhales. I was terrified.

"What to do with her?" said a masculine voice right beside my left ear.

"Leave her," replied another loudly, but from farther away.

"If you leave her, I'm going to take her."

"For what?" asked the first man.

"For a wife. I suspect that underneath that filth she does have a pretty face."

A man snorted. "You only like the filthy ones. Why would you clean her up?"

"She's not one of ours," stated the same man who had suggested leaving me.

They argued back and forth, and I quickly slotted the voices of the four main speakers into convenient nicknames. There was the Questioner, and the Lewd Thinker, and the Loudmouth, and the Old Man.

"What if she's dead?" asked the Questioner.

"She's not," replied the Old Man.

"I'd still take her if she was," said the Lewd Thinker.

"She's a little too fat for my taste," yelled the Loudmouth.

"Better to bear children," the Old Man observed.

"No doubt!" shouted the Loudmouth.

A new voice, gravely, authoritative and cold, cut above the chatter.

"Tie her up? Marry her? Perhaps, first determine if she is crazy, or if she is just lost," suggested Raspy Voice. "And *then* make your decision."

I resisted the urge to open my eyes. This man's words weren't accented like the rest. He sounded exactly like the People.

"Pick her up," he commanded.

Someone reached down and grabbed me, cradling me like a baby. I let my arms and legs hang limply. Whoever was carrying me walked several steps before setting me down gently. It was warm, and I knew that he must've laid me beside the fire.

"Sit her up," Raspy Voice ordered.

Not-too-gentle hands propped me against something, and I felt hands on my mouth, prying it open.

Water, slightly warm and a bit dirty tasting, dribbled down my throat. I swallowed reflexively, and fluttered my eyelids dramatically before opening my eyes and then dropping my jaw in a silent scream. I pressed my lips as far apart as they would go, thrashing my head back and forth while no sound came out. Then I went still, glancing around in wide-eyed terror.

The Old Man bent down and whispered, "You are safe."

A hooded man – the one who was shorter than the rest, and who belonged to the Raspy Voice – crouched beside me. His face and one of his eyes were completely covered by a furry mask. The other eye was cloudy and it stared at me suspiciously from its little opening. I shied away, and shook my head, willing him not to see my blue eyes.

"Who are you?" he demanded.

I shook my head again, this time slowly.

He smacked me across the mouth, and I tasted blood.

My anger spiked, but I forced myself to look sad and confused instead of mad. I lifted my hands and covered my ears. I shook my head as deliberately as I could. Then I brought my hands down over my mouth and shook my head again.

Would they get it?

Please understand, I begged silently.

"I don't think she can hear or speak!" called out Loudmouth.

The man in the mask spun around to give him a glare, seemingly irritated that he hadn't been the one to figure it out.

"That doesn't help us decide what to do with her," he rasped.

He turned back to me, and I tipped my head down to my chest so that I wouldn't have to meet his odd gaze.

"It does make her the perfect woman," the Lewd Thinker stated.

Raspy Voice ignored him. "Feed her, and put her with the prisoner."

"Should we strip her down and wash her, too?"

I heard a shuffle and slap, and I assumed that Raspy Voice had given the Lewd Thinker a whack.

"Is it safe to house her with the prisoner?" the Questioner asked.

"In his tent, she'll be guarded, which works for me. Though I somehow doubt she'll make an attempt to escape," he replied coldly. "And you'll be guarding her for her *own* good. Most of us aren't animals, but that doesn't mean that I want her in a tent with you."

There were murmurs of irritation, and Raspy Voice relented slightly.

"Think of it this way," he said. "Perhaps she will be so grateful to you for saving her, that she might actually bed you of her own free will."

The men laughed, and Raspy Voice turned his attention back to me. He tipped my chin up from its spot on my chest, and I spied a shrewd glint in his cloudy eye. He nodded once, stood up, and strode away.

***

As the men deposited me in the tent, I glanced very quickly at Gavril.

He was asleep – or unconscious, I couldn't tell – under a blanket in the corner.

I scuttled to the opposite end of the tent and cowered there. There still wasn't more than six feet between us, but I thought that putting on a show was a good idea. I eyed Gavril suspiciously, and hugged my knees.

Loudmouth laughed. The man who he was with placed a grimy bowl at my feet, and then they exited together.

I sat quietly, not moving at all. I knew that they must be just outside the flaps, and I didn't want to attract their attention any more than need be. It was cold inside the tent, and I thought that it was probably designed for warmer weather. It was dark, too, and I could hear Gavril's even breathing from across the room. When I was finally sure that the guards weren't returning anytime soon, I grabbed the bowl they'd left, and ate half of its contents. The bread was burnt, and the fish was gritty, but it was still food, and I wasn't going to waste it. I put the rest aside for Gavril.

The guards were silent, and I desperately wanted to see if they were still there. I made my way to the tent flap, holding my breath slightly. I was fully prepared with a phoney faint if I got caught. I flattened myself against the cold ground, and lifted the flap a tiny bit. I couldn't see any boots. I sat up, pushed the doorway open as wide as my hand, and peered outside.

The snow was coming down, and the wind was whipping flurries through the air.

I could see the outline of the two men. They were seated on a sled, which was pushed up against one of the large tents, and they were sound asleep. I smiled. I didn't think that Raspy Voice would be too forgiving of their nap, but I was personally grateful for it. The tent they were leaning against was as dark as the one that I was in, but the third tent, set up on the other side of the fire, was lit from the inside. I closed the tent flap and shuffled toward Gavril.

I leaned over his supine form, and placed my hand on his shoulder. It was warm – almost, but not quite hot – and I was momentarily relieved.

I slid his blanket down a little and hissed involuntarily as I examined his body. His exposed forearm was raw and red. It looked like rope burn.

I moved my gaze up to his face. It was bruised and swollen. His lips were cracked, and there was a decent sized split in the centre of the bottom one.

Oh, God.

My heart hurt, just looking at him.

With a deep breath, I decided to assess the rest the damage. I lifted the blanket up and cringed as I inventoried his wounds.

Scrapes up and down his arms. Ligature marks on his wrists and ankles. Bruises everywhere.

Gavril was clothed in nothing but linen underwear, and most of his torso was black and blue.

I felt tears on my face as I put the blanket down. I sat back for a second. My stomach was queasy. I leaned forward again, placing my cheek beside his mouth so that I could feel his breath on my skin. It was a reassuring sign of life from his otherwise still body. I stayed there for several moments, enjoying the knowledge that if nothing else, at least Gavril was alive.

I started to sit up, and suddenly his lips were on mine. I could taste sweat, and blood. I tried to pull away, but his strong hands found the back of my head, and I surrendered. I ran my fingers along his face, feeling the days old stubble on his chin, and the terrible swelling above one of his eyebrows. He released me to take a breath, and then drew me down again forcefully. His mouth was tender, and swollen, and insistent. I was breathless in moments.

"Gavril," I murmured against his mouth, and he finally let me go.

I pressed my face to his chest, and he went completely still once again. I sat up quickly. His dark eyes, flecked with gold, met my gaze with disbelief.

"Lindsay," he whispered. "It appears that this time I'm not dreaming."

"Gavril."

"Please. Don't marry my brother," he pleaded.

"I won't," I promised.

"Thank you."

He closed his eyes, and I quickly undid my parka and retrieved the battered metal water bottle. I slid my hand under Gavril's head and tipped it up to his mouth. He drank gratefully and smiled at me.

"Lindsay," he whispered again.

"We have to get out of here," I replied urgently.

"Did you bring an army?" he asked in a teasing voice.

I looked at him incredulously. "You're making jokes?"

"I'm naked," he added with a wheezing laugh that dissolved into a cough.

"Not completely," I disagreed with a blush and I pointed to his underwear.

"I'm strong," he said. "But not so much that I will survive outside in this... outfit."

Gavril raised his eyebrows and grinned.

I sighed. I'd been expecting sarcastic comments about my lack of planning. I had assumed that Gavril would be unimpressed that I had decided to rescue him. But I hadn't anticipated humour.

I opened my bag, and glanced nervously at the door flap. I knew that once I started dressing Gavril, there wouldn't be any way to hide my intentions. I pulled the shirt over his head, and Gavril sat up suddenly. His eyes flashed with a little of the irritation I was used to.

It made me feel relieved, and I smiled sweetly at him.

"Calm yourself," I said, and then added in English, "Chivalry is so last season."

For a second, I thought that he might argue, but then he shook his head and let his shoulders drop.

"Good boy," I murmured.

Gavril laughed another choking laugh.

I helped him put his arms into the shirt, and then I smiled. The sleeves were too short, and the length just barely covered his stomach. I gave him some more water, and offered him a handful of the dried granola mixture. He ate it quickly, and I felt bad that I didn't have anything more to offer him. I grabbed the spare pants I'd brought with me, and helped him slide into those, too. They were also too short.

"Did you bring me Andrik's clothes?" he asked.

I grinned, then froze, as Gavril went suddenly still. His gaze was focused on the tent flap.

"Lie down," I commanded in a hiss, and he obeyed.

I covered him to his chin with the blanket and dove back to my corner. I sprawled out awkwardly, feigning sleep. Cold hair blew into the tent as someone entered.

"Waste of time," muttered the Old Man.

"Why don't we just kill them now?" the Questioner wanted to know.

"This man is the Gavril the Slayer," the Old Man replied.

"I know. So why don't we kill him?"

The Old Man sighed. "We will. When we reach the village."

"What difference does it make?"

"This man killed Silv's son and only heir. It is Silv's right to do with him as he sees fit."

The Questioner was silent for a moment.

"What about the girl?" he finally said.

"What about her?"

"What purpose does she serve?"

"I don't know," the Old Man replied. "But our unfortunate leader has chosen to let her live."

"I'm tired of taking orders from one of their People," the Questioner muttered.

"Me, too," agreed the Old Man. "Perhaps when we're done with him, Silv will let you kill him."

They both laughed.

I heard a sharp smack, and then a groan from Gavril.

Both of the other men laughed again.

"Should we wake the guards?" asked the Questioner.

"No," replied the Old Man. "Let him deal with them."

Then they were gone in another blast of air.

"Are you all right?" I whispered as soon as I could breathe again.

When Gavril didn't answer immediately, I sat up and made my way to his side.

"I'll be fine. But I'm sore in many places," he admitted quietly.

"I want to kill them," I said angrily.

Gavril squeezed my hand.

"I'll be able to walk, at least for a little while," he told me. "They do seem to prefer hitting in the face or the chest."

I touched the fresh red mark on his cheek, wondering which of the two men had done it.

"I may never be my handsome self again," Gavril joked.

"You're beautiful," I replied.

He reached up and pulled me down to kiss me. His fingers twined with my ash-covered hair and his thumbs circled the back of my neck, drawing out a moan before I forced myself to pull away.

"We have to go," I breathed. "Before they come back again."

"Okay." He kissed me again with only slightly less fervor.

"The fact that you're so agreeable worries me," I told him.

He grinned. "No, Lindsay, we must stay here."

"Better."

"Thank you."

I stared at him critically, wondering if I could somehow rig my sleeping gear into a coat. I would've given him my own if I thought he would be able to stretch it across his wide shoulders. But I knew it wouldn't work. And I knew what my only option was.

I took a breath before I told him. "Gavril. I'm going to have to steal a jacket and some boots."

"No."

"I'll be careful and I'll come right back."

He started to protest again, and I silenced him with a kiss.

I buttoned up my parka and slipped out into the snowstorm. The two men who were supposed to be guarding us were still huddled on the sled, and they were still asleep. I pressed my body against the small tent and slid along its surface until I reached the edge, then I dove toward the larger structure. I held my ear against the leather, listening for movement from inside. I couldn't hear anything, so I slunk over to the door flap and eased my way in.

I sunk to the ground.

Someone inside was snoring loudly.

But I could see a pile of gear, just out of my reach.

With a shaking body, I crept toward it and snaked a hand out to grab two boots and a coat.

I froze again as the snorer shifted in his bed.

Please, I thought.

The man shifted once again, then settled.

I tucked the boots and coat under my arm and crawled backward out of the tent. I stood carefully, then dove once again to the smaller tent. I crept along to the flap, and slid inside, where I promptly burst into tears.

Gavril stood up with a perplexed look on his face. I tossed him the gear.

"Put those on," I whispered.

The tightness in my chest eased slightly as he put the boots on. They were tall enough to meet the bottom of his pants, and when he slipped the parka on, it fit perfectly. He gritted his teeth each time the fur brushed one of his cuts.

"Does it hurt badly?" I ask.

"Yes."

His face was pale under his naturally tanned skin, and I felt sick about taking him out in the cold.

"There's a storm out there," I warned.

Gavril pulled his hood up, wincing as it caught on his fresh wound.

"Let's go," he said in English, and smiled a little.

"One more thing," I replied.

I grabbed the leather rope from the bag and tied us together at the wrist.

I guided him outside, pointing at the sleeping guards as we sneaked by. I pulled the compass out of my pocket and strained to see it.

"East," I murmured.

I inhaled nervously, and took a step out into the open tundra. The wind whipped us hard, and I felt Gavril tense up behind me. I pushed aside my worry. We had to keep moving.

I had no idea how long it was going to take the men from the camp to notice that we were missing, but I wanted a good head start.

I pushed on, glancing at my compass and trying not to fall, and making sure that Gavril was keeping up. The storm didn't abate, and I walked on blindly until I felt a sharp tug on the leather rope. I stopped and turned to face him. He pulled the rope again, and gestured for me to come closer. I stepped in so that our foreheads almost met. A sheen of sweat covered his whole face.

"Lindsay," he said. "Those men are as unused to this kind of cold as you are. And they're not half as brave."

"But they're at least determined, and far more stupid," I countered.

"I don't think they'll come after us until after the storm has passed," Gavril stated.

"I know how badly they want you," I replied softly.

He looked like he was going to argue, but then he just sighed. "Who told you?"

"Nanaj."

"Of course she did," he muttered. "Lindsay…I'm too tired to travel much further. And if we continue, I won't have the strength to build us the shelter we'll need."

"Okay," I agreed. "Let's stop."

Relief flooded Gavril's face, and I felt bad for having pushed him so hard.

"What do you see on the horizon?" he asked.

"I don't even see a horizon," I said.

He smiled. "The item you've been using to guide us, can it get us back on track if we stray?"

"Sure."

"Do you mind following me for while?" he asked.

"Sure," I said again.

Gavril glanced left, then right, and set off. I didn't know what he saw, but I followed him for five full minutes before we stopped. He kicked a wide snowdrift and nodded with satisfaction.

"Do you have a shovel?" he wanted to know.

"No."

"Something to dig with?"

I grabbed my bag, reached in and pulled out the mirror.

"It will do," Gavril told me.

He undid the leather rope, and got to work.

He dug under the drift, piling small amounts of snow on top, and smoothing the hole as he went. He did it methodically. *Scoop. Pat down. Scoop. Pat down.*

"Can I help?" I asked.

"Keep watch," he suggested. "And please dig me out if it collapses."

"Will that happen?"

"No." I could hear the smile in his voice.

He was remarkably efficient, and before long, his digging had amounted to a smooth mound of snow that was four feet high at its peak, and one foot thick at its crest. It was as long as Gavril himself, and as he dug, he disappeared inside.

"Are you okay?" I called.

He slid out, and gave me a tired smile.

"Now we wait," he said.

"For what?"

"The snow to set." Gavril looked up at the sky. "It's very cold. It won't take long."

We waited in silence, with the flakes falling around us. My thoughts tumbled loosely around in my head.

Taras and his disbelieving face.

Nanaj, caring for her injured husband.

My life at home.

And even Ben.

I wanted to say something, but I didn't know where to start.

The snow built up on the fur brim of Gavril's stolen parka, and I reached up to brush it away. He grabbed my mitten-covered hand and held it tightly.

"Now," he said gruffly, and stood up to go back to work.

He shuffled back into his frozen cave, and after a moment, handfuls of snow came flying out.

"Come in," he suggested, sounding muffled.

I crouched down and peered inside. It looked dark, and suffocating, and I couldn't see Gavril at all.

"Hello?" I called.

He laughed. "It's safe."

"So you say," I muttered.

"I promise you," he said in a thick voice.

I crawled into the dugout snowdrift, pushed my way past a pile of snow, and realized that it was actually a decent size. There was enough room to sit up, and in the dark, I could see Gavril resting against a curved wall with my bag in his hand.

"Wow," I said.

"Wow?" he repeated.

"Exactly."

"We still need to seal ourselves in, and we need to make a ventilation hole," he told me. "You don't happen to have a spear?"

"Nope. But I do have this."

I pulled the collapsible walking stick out and handed it to him.

"Good. Pile the remaining snow in the entryway, and I'll make the hole," Gavril said.

As I used the mirror to move the snow, Gavril worked the walking stick through the ceiling. When I was almost done, he took off his parka and used it to fill in the rest of the gap in the doorway, then leaned back in the dark. It was pitch black inside for just a moment, then I heard a snap, and the cave was bathed in orange light. Gavril held up his makeshift candle with a smile.

It was the jar of jelly-like stuff I'd tossed into the bag, topped with a piece of my linen rope.

He set my flint and the candle onto a little shelf he'd dug into the wall and sighed. His face was more tired than it had been when I'd first found him in the tent.

"You need to rest," I said.

I put my bedroll on the floor and unrolled the fur sleeping bag. I pointed at the bedding, and unbuttoned my parka. Gavril pulled his too-small tunic over his head, kicked off his boots, and stretched out directly onto the snowy floor.

It was impossible to look anywhere but him.

His wide chest was bruised and battered, but its hulking, muscular form took up most of the space. And all of my vision.

"Your turn," he teased.

"Nice try," I said.

But I was tempted. Very tempted. Especially when he smiled and rolled so that he was taking up half of the bed.

"Join me," he suggested.

"Um. No."

"Are you scared?"

He didn't sound like he was kidding, so I answered him with equal honesty.

"Terrified."

"Of me?" His question was most un-Gavril-like.

"Of how you make me feel," I confessed.

He smiled, and the gold flecks in his eyes danced with pleasure. But at that moment, I noticed that his eyes were also very glassy. And his cheeks were flushed.

"I think you're sick."

I moved closer so I could place the back of my hand on his neck. It was burning hot.

I sat up quickly, grabbed my bag and dug through it until I found the pill bottle. I dumped the contents into my hand. There were two Advils and eight prescription pills that I thought might be Amoxicillin.

"Do you trust me?" I asked.

He didn't answer me.

"Gavril?"

I turned back to him, and his eyes were closed. I squeezed his forearm and he didn't budge.

"Hey," I said softly, right beside his ear.

He groaned and rolled onto his back. I pressed my head to his chest. There was a thick rattle as he breathed in and out.

"Can you hear me?" I raised my voice a little.

"Sorry," he said. "I think I fell asleep."

"It's okay."

"Hurts a bit to breathe," he told me.

"Why didn't you say something before?"

He offered me a horizontal shrug. "I guess I had more important things on my mind."

"You're a good healer," I told him. "But a bad patient."

He smiled weakly. "Thank you."

"I need you to sit up a bit."

He propped himself up with a bit of difficulty. I handed him the water bottle, the Advil, and two of the antibiotics.

"I need you to trust me. And I need you to swallow these," I said.

He tossed them into his mouth without hesitation, then gulped down some water.

"And now?" he wondered out loud.

"Sleep," I suggested.

"If you will, too," he agreed. "Lie down."

He rolled to his side, and then raised his arm. And this time, I was more scared of *not* joining him. At least if I was lying beside him, I could act like a human thermometer. So I blew out the little light and curled up underneath his arm. In just a few moments he was sound asleep.

I was restless, but I didn't dare move for fear of waking Gavril. It took a long while, but I finally dozed, and when I did, a dream of heavy-footed men marching over our sleeping bodies woke me. I stirred and listened to Gavril's breathing. I drifted again, and imagined that I could hear the storm raging outside the cave, before entering a more restful state.

***

When I woke up, our little cave was utterly silent, and I was chilly.

"Gavril?" I whispered, and as I stretched out, I realized that he wasn't curled around me anymore.

I sat up, and suddenly the cave lit up again.

"I'm here," he replied softly. "Adjusting the ventilation. And thinking about breakfast."

"Is it morning?" I asked.

Gavril shrugged. "I'm hungry."

"I don't have much left," I admitted.

"I see that."

He had two pieces of dried meat in his hand, and the last of the granola sitting in its bag on his lap.

"Eat it all," I told him.

"I really don't think so," he replied, and tossed me a piece of meat. "I could hunt."

I remembered his rattling chest.

"How do you feel?" I asked.

"Very good. Let's eat."

"I want you to take two more of these," I told him, and handed him the bottle of pills.

He dry-swallowed them without asking what they were, and reached into the granola. I placed my hand on the back of his neck again. It was definitely cooler, and I smiled. He paused mid-scoop and looked me in the eye.

"Tell me," he said.

I didn't need to ask for clarification.

"I thought you were dead," I replied.

"Why?"

"Taras's words."

Gavril's face darkened.

"Maybe I took what he said the wrong way," I amended.

"My brother does everything that he does with the greatest of purpose."

"I know," I replied softly. "And he left you."

"But *you* didn't."

"I couldn't."

"No."

"Taras truly believed that they were going to kill you," I added.

"Why are you defending him?" Gavril demanded.

Why, indeed? But I knew the answer. I wasn't defending Taras at all. I was defending my own actions.

Gavril read my expression, and he realized it, too. His eyes flashed angrily for a second, and I thought he might tear through the snow walls and storm off. But instead he leaned very slowly toward me and kissed my forehead.

"I want you to be mine, Lindsay," he said. "But freely."

Even though the two words were at odds with each other, even though being possessed by someone else seemed like the antithesis of freedom…It's what I wanted, too. To give myself to this bristly, unpredictable man who'd risked his life to save mine, and for whom I'd done the same. And that terrified me.

Gavril reached for me and cupped my cheek gently in his palm.

"You're letting yourself be scared because you think being scared is the easy way out, Lindsay. Trust me. No one knows it better than I do. I've been scared since the moment we met. I ran from it too. But if I'd just faced it head-on before…" He trailed off and cleared his throat. "But I couldn't face *that* fear until I had to face something that scared me even more."

"What was that?"

"The thought of losing you. Of never telling you how *I* feel. Of never getting to show you."

His words overwhelmed me. "I don't want that either."

Gavril's answering stare was tense with need. "What *do* you want, Lindsay?"

"You."

He pulled me closer, and suddenly it was I who was too warm instead of him.

"Jacket," he ordered.

I shrugged it off, barely getting both arms out before he grabbed my face and trailed kissed from my lips to my chin to my neck.

"Shirt," he commanded.

I let him lift the tunic over my head, and I covered myself self-consciously. He drew my arms away from my chest and his eyes raked over me hungrily. I shivered in anticipation of the fact that his hands would soon be following his gaze.

I wanted him to hurry. But I wanted him to go slowly, too.

When he reached for me again, I shivered again.

"Are you cold?" he asked softly.

I almost laughed. I felt like every part of my body was on fire. I covered my mouth and shook my head.

"Far from cold."

"Good," he said, and drew me down onto the makeshift bed so that we were lying facing each other.

Then Gavril pulled my hand to his face, and kissed me gently. He pressed his body against mine, hard lines meeting my exposed curves. When his skin touched mine, I gasped, and he pulled back.

"You're okay?" he wanted to know.

"I'm perfect," I said, and pulled him back down.

He kissed me again, this time more urgently. He slid his hands underneath my pants and shimmied them down gently. I had less self-control, and ripped Gavril's pants at the seams as I tried to yank them down. He laughed into my mouth as it happened, and his body vibrated pleasantly with the sound. He pulled the pants off himself, but left on the linen underwear.

He kissed me. Sweetly. Then heatedly. Then with ownership. He traced my lips with his tongue, and I let him explore. I savored the feeling of being claimed.

"Tell me again," he murmured against my mouth.

"Tell you what?"

"That you want me."

"I want you, Gavril." I said it in the People's language first, and again in English, then added, "I've never wanted anything so badly, never been surer of something."

It was true. Not an ounce of doubt remained. Only passion and need.

"Me too," Gavril said, his voice thick with matching desire.

He silenced his voice then, but not his hands. With his fingers, he traced the length of my body – mid-thigh to hip to elbow to shoulder. Then he lifted my arm above my head and did same. Collarbone to breast to stomach. He paused at my belly button, slipped his hand between my thighs, and found me waiting. Wanting. But he wasn't done exploring.

He took my other hand and raised it up too, then used his mouth to follow the trail his fingers had created. Forehead to mouth to breast to thigh. Then back again. Each kiss made me gasp, each taste made me squirm. By the time he got back to my mouth, I was alight with want.

"Is this the same, where you live?" Gavril asked softly.

I closed my hand over his. "I live here, Gavril. And nothing has ever been like this. Not for me."

My answer seemed to satisfy him. He slipped off his underwear – the final barrier between us – and positioned himself above me.

"Lindsay," he whispered. "Please say you'll be my wife."

In response, I pulled his mouth to mine, hooked a leg over his hips, and drew him into me. In moments, I forgot the icy cave and the imminent danger outside of it. I forgot that I'd lived anywhere but in the Village, then forgot about the Village itself.

As Gavril filled me, sending my internal spiral higher and higher, winding me up tighter and tighter, I forgot everything.

Everything but him.

Just when I was sure I couldn't climb to a greater height, that I couldn't hold on any longer, Gavril tensed above me. And inside me. And I lost myself completely as we found release together.

***

I slept deeply, and when I woke up, I opened my eyes slowly, enjoying the idea that I could roll over and touch Gavril. The fur sleeping bag was draped over my shoulders, and I felt altogether good.

"Are you awake?" I whispered.

He didn't answer me.

"Gavril?"

I sat up, realizing that he had woken before me yet again. I blinked, and I saw that the cave was lit by a sliver of natural light.

I breathed in, and fresh, cold air tingled pleasantly in my chest. I disentangled myself from the thin blanket and got dressed quickly.

"Gavril?" I called, a little more loudly.

He still didn't reply. I put on my parka and my boots, and I saw that he had dug out the entry-way, then propped my bag against the opening. I grabbed it and crawled out of the cave. I could smell fire and roasting meat. My mouth watered.

"Where are you?" I wondered out loud as I looked around.

A small bird hung on a spit over a low fire.

"I don't know what that bird was doing all the way inland, but it will make an excellent lunch, hmm?" said a mocking and raspy voice.

I spun around.

And I almost fell over.

Raspy Voice was sitting there casually with Gavril's head in his lap. He was also holding a bone knife to Gavril's throat.

"I see that you still don't recognize me," he said. "Gavril didn't at first, either. Tell her."

Raspy Voice moved the knife ever so slightly, and Gavril winced as a drop of blood appeared under his Adam's apple.

"Please, stop," I whispered.

"Pardon me? I didn't quite hear you," Raspy Voice stated. "Or maybe that's just because you were mute a day and a half ago."

"Don't hurt him," I begged.

Raspy Voice kept the knife where it was. "Tell her."

"Lindsay," Gavril said in a strained voice. "You remember Elak."

I frowned, and Raspy Voice laughed. He pulled off his hood and his mask, and I saw that his face was covered in badly healed burns.

Nanaj's abusive husband.

"I'm afraid I had a bit of a run-in with the Outsiders. They wanted information about our mutual friend here. I told them what they wanted to know, but they punished me anyway, just for being one of the People. It's unfortunate that Gavril kicked me out of the Village and gave my wife away when he did. I never did manage to catch up to the Guard."

"It's not his fault," I started to say, but I cut myself off when Elak kneed Gavril in the back.

"It's rude to interrupt," he said. "May I carry on?"

I nodded nervously.

"Good." He smiled. "Once they had cheerfully maimed me beyond recognition, they decided to give me a job. They wanted me to lure Gavril out, to capture him, and to bring him to their village. Where they'd no doubt kill him. And then me."

I was silent. I didn't want Gavril to receive any more punishment on my behalf.

Disappointment flashed across Elak's face.

"I agreed to help them anyway, but on my own conditions. I asked permission to train their men," he told me. "Can you believe that they don't bother? They just assume that it is their right to win. Their self-righteousness is astounding, really. Would you agree?"

I didn't know whether to answer or not, and Elak wasn't giving me any indication.

"Yes," I finally whispered, and he carried on.

"I had a very short period of time to train them, but I did what I could. Do you know what my second condition was?"

I shook my head.

"I wanted permission to go after *you*," he laughed. "Imagine how delighted I was when you came to me instead. It took me the better part of a day to figure out who you were, though. Clever disguise, I'll admit. But I knew that you weren't one of our People. Yet, you still looked familiar. Then I put it together. And I realized how much happier I'd be if I was guaranteed my revenge first, before giving over Gavril. If I'm going to die, I might as well die happy."

I said nothing.

"Do you have rope in that bag?" Elak asked.

I nodded.

"Get it," he ordered.

I reached into the bag, and my hand hit the metal of the gun. My heart raced, and I pushed the weapon aside to grab the rope.

"Toss it to me," Elak said.

I did, then watched as he hogtied Gavril and pushed him down into the snow.

"I might still take him to their village," he said thoughtfully. "But not until I've taken you from him."

"No," Gavril protested, and Elak kicked him in the ribs.

"A wife for a wife, right?" he laughed.

I took a step back, and Elak lunged for me. I side stepped him, and watched in surprise as he went down. He got up quickly, and eyed me a little more warily. Had he thought that I was just going to let him kill me?

He jumped at me again, fists out. I stepped back again, not quite quickly enough this time. One of his hands grazed my shoulder painfully. He stepped toward me once more, smiling. He aimed for my head, and missed.

"Hit him!" Gavril yelled.

I swung my bag at Elak, and he laughed. Until it hit the side of his head. There was a solid thud as the gun struck him, and he stumbled backward.

"Good!" Gavril called.

"Fine," Elak snarled. "Make it hard."

He pulled the bone knife out of his pocket and stalked toward Gavril.

I fumbled to get the gun out, hoping that it didn't have a safety, praying that it was loaded. I held it up with shaking hands and aimed it at Elak's back.

"Stop!" I shouted.

He ignored me, and drew the knife back.

"Don't!" I screamed.

He turned to smile at me, then dove at Gavril. I watched the knife sink into Gavril's skin, just below his neck.

And I pulled the trigger.

The gun kicked back, and the sound was deafening. I didn't see the bullet hit him, but I saw the spray of blood hit the snow. I sank to my knees, sobbing uncontrollably.

Elak didn't move. But neither did Gavril.

My ears were ringing as they had right after the plane crash, and soon my vision was too blurred by tears to see straight.

"Lindsay."

I covered my ears, trying to clear away the voice.

"Lindsay.""

Leave me alone, I thought.

"Lindsay!"

The sudden urgency made my head snap up, searching for the source.

Gavril.

He was still lying on the snow with his arms and legs tied behind his back. I forced myself to my feet and walked woodenly toward him. His eyes were open, and he was watching me curiously. I maneuvered around Elak's still form, then untied Gavril quickly, and pulled the knife out. It wasn't more than half an inch deep. I tossed the knife aside, and took a shaky breath.

"Lindsay?"

"I'm sorry," I said.

He put his arms around me, and I leaned into his chest.

"You did what you had to do," he told me softly. "Even if I don't know exactly what it was."

"I'm sorry," I said.

"Don't be. Elak wasn't a good man."

"I'm not sorry about Elak," I replied. "I'm sorry that I hesitated."

I touched his new wound gingerly. The blood was already starting to dry.

"It looks worse than it feels," he assured me. "I'll heal quickly."

"Gavril," I said. "I love you."

"I love you, too," he replied, and squeezed me tightly.

"If the snow should melt, and the sea should overtake the land, still I will stand beside you," I whispered.

"Lindsay?"

"If the stars should fall from the sky, and the earth split open to swallow them whole, still I will stand beside you," I continued.

"Do you know what you're saying?" Gavril asked.

I nodded, and I went on. "I will stand beside you until the moment I can stand no longer."

Gavril didn't hesitate.

"If your body or soul should grow weary, I shall carry you," he said formally. "If your steps falter, I shall lift you up. If you stumble, I shall steady you. From this moment forward, I pledge my heart to yours."

"And mine to yours," I replied.

He kissed me lovingly.

"Good," I said wearily. "Now, my husband, will you please take me home?"

"There's nothing I'd love more."

Epilogue

"It's still a shame you ruined the other dress," Nanaj teased.

I grinned at her.

"I would like to have seen Satu's face when she found it."

"No," my friend disagreed. "You really wouldn't have liked to have seen that. Andrik brought it to her in pieces. I have *never* seen someone's face go that shade of green. I thought she was going to be sick right then and there."

I laughed. "You have to admit, this dress suits me better, anyway."

"And you made it yourself," Nanaj reminded me proudly.

I touched the soft purple edging, woven carefully through the near-to-white linen. It had taken me hours to trim the fabric from my old blouse, and a painstaking day and a half to stitch the edges perfectly, so that they wouldn't fray. I had sewn an empire waist, and an A-line skirt, and I had been too afraid to ask Satu for any help.

"It is pretty, isn't it?" I bragged.

Lanka's voice came from the doorway. "It's beautiful. Though not traditional."

"Thank you," I replied. "To both those things."

"Will you excuse us, Nanaj?"

Nanaj made a final adjustment to my hair – it was loose, and a little frizzy, and covered in clusters of purple flowers, attached by their leathery stems. She kissed my cheek and left the room.

"You've made a good choice," Lanka told me.

"Is Taras very angry?" I asked.

"Not at all," she replied. "He values ambition over love, but that doesn't mean he doesn't value it at all."

I felt myself blushing.

"I'm just glad he no longer thinks I'm the woman in the story," I said.

"No one said that," Lanka stated.

"What?"

She gave me a speculative look.

"Some men are born into leadership, and some are forced into it by circumstance," she told me. "The story may not have been about my second son at all."

I stared at her.

"From what I understand, this ceremony is just a formality. You've already said the words," she reminded me. "So running away will do you no good, either."

"I'm not going anywhere."

She nodded with satisfaction. "Well then, I'll leave you to it."

Lanka gave me her nearly toothless grin, and she was gone before I could respond.

Made in the USA
Charleston, SC
31 January 2016